The VAMPIRE DIARIES
THE STRUGGLE

The VAMPIRE DIARIES
THE STRUGGLE

L.J. SMITH

Hodder
Children's
Books

a division of Hodder Headline Limited

Text copyright © 1991 Daniel Weiss Associates, Inc. and Lisa J Smith

First published in the USA in 1991
by HarperPaperbacks, an imprint of HarperCollins Publishers Inc.

First published in Great Britain in 2001
by Hodder Children's Books

The right of Lisa J Smith to be identified as the Author of
this Work has been asserted by her in accordance with
the Copyright, Designs and Patents Act 1988.

10 9 8 7 6 5 4 3 2 1

A Catalogue record for this book is available
from the British Library

ISBN 0 340 84350 0

Typeset by Avon Dataset Ltd, Bidford-on-Avon, Warks

Printed and bound in Great Britain by
Clays Ltd, St Ives plc

Hodder Children's Books
a division of Hodder Headline Ltd
338 Euston Road
London NW1 3BH

To my dear friend and sister, Judy

A special thanks to Anne Smith, Peggy Bokulic,
Anne Marie Smith, and Laura Penny
for information about Virginia, and to
Jack and Sue Check for all their local lore.

CHAPTER
1

"Damon!"

Icy wind whipped Elena's hair around her face, tearing at her light sweater. Oak leaves swirled among the rows of granite headstones, and the trees lashed their branches together in a frenzy. Elena's hands were cold, her lips and cheeks numb, but she stood facing the screaming wind directly, shouting into it.

"Damon!"

This weather was a show of his Power, meant to frighten her away. It wouldn't work. The thought of that same Power being turned against Stefan woke a hot fury inside her that burned against the wind. If Damon had done anything to Stefan, if Damon had hurt him . . .

"Damn you, answer me!" she shouted at the oak trees that bordered the graveyard.

A dead oak leaf like a withered brown hand skittered up to her foot, but there was no answer. Above, the sky was as grey as glass, as grey as the tombstones that surrounded her. Elena felt rage and frustration sting her throat and she sagged. She'd been wrong. Damon wasn't here after all; she was alone with the screaming wind.

She turned – and gasped.

He was just behind her, so close that her clothes brushed his as she turned. At that distance, she should have sensed another human being standing there, should have felt his body warmth or heard him. But Damon, of course, wasn't human.

She reeled back a couple of steps before she could stop herself. Every instinct that had lain quiet while she shouted into the violence of the wind was now begging her to run.

She clenched her fists. "Where's Stefan?"

A line appeared between Damon's dark eyebrows. "Stefan who?"

Elena stepped forward and slapped him.

She had no thought of doing it before she did it, and afterwards she could scarcely believe what she had done. But it was a good hard slap, with the full force of her body behind it, and it snapped Damon's head to one side. Her hand stung. She stood, trying to calm her breath, and watched him.

He was dressed as she had first seen him, in black. Soft black boots, black jeans, black sweater, and leather jacket. And he looked like Stefan. She didn't know how she could have missed that before. He had the same dark hair, the same pale skin, the same disturbing good looks. But his hair was straight, not wavy, and his eyes were black as midnight, and his mouth was cruel.

He turned his head slowly back to look at her, and she saw blood rising in the cheek she'd slapped.

"Don't lie to me," she said, her voice shaking. "I know who you are. I know *what* you are. You killed Mr Tanner last night. And now Stefan's disappeared."

"Has he?"

"You know he has!"

Damon smiled, and then turned it off instantly.

"I'm warning you; if you've hurt him—"

"Then, what?" he said. "What will you do, Elena? What *can* you do, against me?"

Elena fell silent. For the first time, she realised that the wind had died away. The day had gone deadly quiet around them, as if they stood motionless at the centre of some great circle of power. It seemed as if everything, the leaden sky, the oaks and purple beeches, the ground itself, was connected to him, as if he drew Power from all of it. He stood with his head tilted back slightly, his eyes fathomless and full of strange lights.

"I don't know," she whispered, "but I'll find something. Believe me."

He laughed suddenly, and Elena's heart jerked and began pounding hard. God, he was beautiful. Handsome was too weak and colourless a word. As usual, the laughter lasted only a moment, but even when his lips had sobered it left traces in his eyes.

"I do believe you," he said, relaxing, looking around the graveyard. Then he turned back and held out a hand to her. "You're too good for my brother," he said casually.

Elena thought of slapping the hand away, but she didn't want to touch him again. "Tell me where he is."

"Later, possibly – for a price." He withdrew his hand, just as Elena realised that on it he wore a ring like Stefan's: silver and lapis lazuli. Remember that, she thought fiercely. It's important.

"My brother," he went on, "is a fool. He thinks that because you look like Katherine you're weak and easily led like her. But he's wrong. I could feel your anger from the other side of town. I can feel it now, a white light like the desert sun. You have strength, Elena, even as you are. But you could be so much stronger . . ."

She stared at him, not understanding, not liking the change of subject. "I don't know what you're talking about. And what has it got to do with Stefan?"

"I'm talking about Power, Elena." Suddenly, he stepped close to her, his eyes fixed on hers, his voice soft and urgent. "You've tried everything else, and nothing has satisfied you. You're the girl who has everything, but there's always been something just out of your reach, something you need desperately and can't have. That's what I'm offering you. Power. Eternal life. And feelings you've never felt before."

She *did* understand then, and bile rose in her throat.

She choked on horror and repudiation. "No."

"Why not?" he whispered. "Why not try it, Elena? Be honest. Isn't there a part of you that wants to?" His dark eyes were full of a heat and intensity that held her transfixed, unable to look away. "I can waken things inside you that have been sleeping all your life. You're strong enough to live in the dark, to glory in it. You can become a queen of the shadows. Why not take that Power, Elena? Let me help you take it."

"*No*," she said, wrenching her eyes away from his. She wouldn't look at him, wouldn't let him do this to her. She wouldn't let him make her forget . . . make her forget . . .

"It's the ultimate secret, Elena," he said. His voice was as caressing as the fingertips that touched her throat. "You'll be happy as never before."

There was something terribly important she must remember. He was using Power to make her forget it, but she wouldn't let him make her forget . . .

"And we'll be together, you and I." The cool fingertips stroked the side of her neck, slipping under the collar of her sweater. "Just the two of us, for ever."

There was a sudden twinge of pain as his fingers brushed two tiny wounds in the flesh of her neck, and her mind cleared.

Make her forget . . . *Stefan*.

That was what he wanted to drive out of her mind. The memory of Stefan, of his green eyes and his smile that always had sadness lurking behind it. But nothing could force Stefan out of her thoughts now, not after what they had shared. She pulled away from Damon, knocking those cool fingertips aside. She looked straight at him.

"I've already found what I want," she said brutally. "And who I want to be with for ever."

Blackness welled up in his eyes, a cold rage that swept through the air between them. Looking into those eyes, Elena thought of a cobra about to strike.

"Don't you be as stupid as my brother is," he said. "Or I might have to treat you the same way."

She was frightened now. She couldn't help it, not with cold pouring into her, chilling her bones. The wind was picking up again, the branches tossing. "Tell me where he is, Damon."

"At this moment? I don't know. Can't you stop thinking about him for an instant?"

"No!" She shuddered, hair lashing about her face again.

"And that's your final answer, today? Be very sure you want to play this game with me, Elena. The consequences are nothing to laugh about."

"I *am* sure." She had to stop him before he got to her again. "And you can't intimidate me, Damon, or haven't you noticed? The moment Stefan told me what you were, what you'd done, you lost any power you might have had over me. I *hate* you. You disgust me. And there's nothing you can do to me, not any more."

His face altered, the sensuousness twisting and freezing, becoming cruel and bitterly hard. He laughed, but this laugh went on and on. "Nothing?" he said. "I can do *anything* to you, and to the ones you love. You have no idea, Elena, of what I can do. But you'll learn."

He stepped back, and the wind cut through Elena like a knife. Her vision seemed to be blurring – it was as if flecks of brightness filled the air in front of her eyes.

"Winter is coming, Elena," he said, and his voice was clear and chilling even over the howl of the wind. "An unforgiving season. Before it comes, you'll have learned what I can and can't do. Before winter is here, you'll have joined me. You'll be mine."

The swirling whiteness was blinding her, and she could no longer see the dark bulk of his figure. Now even his voice was fading. She hugged herself with her arms, head bent down, her whole body shaking. She whispered, "Stefan—"

"Oh, and one more thing," Damon's voice came back. "You asked earlier about my brother. Don't bother looking for him, Elena. I killed him last night."

Her head jerked up, but there was nothing to see, only the dizzying whiteness, which burned her nose and cheeks and clogged her eyelashes. It was only then, as the fine grains settled on her skin, that she realised what they were: snowflakes.

It was snowing on the first of November. Overhead, the sun was gone.

CHAPTER

An unnatural twilight hung over the abandoned graveyard. Snow blurred Elena's eyes, and the wind numbed her body as if she'd stepped into a current of icy water. Nevertheless, stubbornly, she did not turn around towards the modern cemetery and the road beyond it. As best she could judge, Wickery Bridge was straight in front of her. She headed for that.

The police had found Stefan's abandoned car by Old Creek Road. That meant he'd left it somewhere between Drowning Creek and the woods. Elena stumbled on the overgrown path through the graveyard, but she kept moving, head down, arms hugging her light sweater to her. She had known this graveyard all her life, and she could find her way through it blind.

By the time she crossed the bridge, her shivering

had become painful. It wasn't snowing as hard now, but the wind was even worse. It cut through her clothes as if they were made of tissue paper, and took her breath away.

Stefan, she thought, and turned on to Old Creek Road, trudging northwards. She didn't believe what Damon had said. If Stefan were dead she would *know*. He was alive, somewhere, and she had to find him. He could be anywhere out in this swirling whiteness; he could be hurt, freezing. Dimly, Elena sensed that she was no longer rational. All her thoughts had narrowed down to one single idea. Stefan. Find Stefan.

It was getting harder to keep to the road. On her right were oak trees, on her left, the swift waters of Drowning Creek. She staggered and slowed. The wind didn't seem quite so bad any more, but she did feel very tired. She needed to sit down and rest, just for a minute.

As she sank down beside the road, she suddenly realised how silly she had been to go out searching for Stefan. Stefan would come to her. All she needed to do was sit here and wait. He was probably coming right now.

Elena shut her eyes and leaned her head against her drawn-up knees. She felt much warmer now. Her mind drifted and she saw Stefan, saw him smile at her. His arms around her were strong and secure, and she relaxed against him, glad to let go of fear and tension. She was home. She was where she belonged. Stefan would never let anything hurt her.

But then, instead of holding her, Stefan was shaking

her. He was ruining the beautiful tranquility of her rest. She saw his face, pale and urgent, his green eyes dark with pain. She tried to tell him to be still, but he wouldn't listen. *Elena, get up*, he said, and she felt the compelling force of those green eyes willing her to do it. *Elena, get up now—*

"Elena, get up!" The voice was high and thin and frightened. "Come on, Elena! Get up! We can't carry you!"

Blinking, Elena brought a face into focus. It was small and heart-shaped, with fair, almost translucent skin, framed by masses of soft red curls. Wide brown eyes, with snowflakes caught in the lashes, stared worriedly into hers.

"Bonnie," she said slowly. "What are you doing here?"

"Helping me look for you," said a second, lower voice on Elena's other side. She turned slightly to see elegantly arched eyebrows and an olive complexion. Meredith's dark eyes, usually so ironic, were worried now, too. "Stand up, Elena, unless you want to become an ice princess for real."

There was snow all over her, like a white fur coat. Stiffly, Elena stood, leaning heavily on the two other girls. They walked her back to Meredith's car.

It should have been warmer inside the car, but Elena's nerve endings were coming back to life, making her shake, telling her how cold she really was. Winter is an unforgiving season, she thought as Meredith drove.

"What's going on, Elena?" said Bonnie from the

back seat. "What did you think you were doing, running away from school like that? And how could you come out *here*?"

Elena hesitated, then shook her head. She wanted nothing more than to tell Bonnie and Meredith everything. To tell them the whole terrifying story about Stefan and Damon and what had really happened last night to Mr Tanner – and about after. But she couldn't. Even if they would believe her, it wasn't her secret to tell.

"Everyone's out looking for you," Meredith said. "The whole school's upset, and your aunt was nearly frantic."

"Sorry," said Elena dully, trying to stop her violent shivering. They turned on to Maple Street and pulled up to her house.

Aunt Judith was waiting inside with heated blankets. "I knew if they found you, you'd be half-frozen," she said in a determinedly cheerful voice as she reached for Elena. "Snow on the day after Hallowe'en! I can hardly believe it. Where did you girls find her?"

"On Old Creek Road, past the bridge," said Meredith.

Aunt Judith's thin face lost colour. "Near the graveyard? Where the attacks were? Elena, how *could* you . . . ?" Her voice trailed off as she looked at Elena. "We won't say anything more about it right now," she said, trying to regain her cheerful manner. "Let's get you out of those wet clothes."

"I have to go back once I'm dry," said Elena. Her

brain was working again, and one thing was clear: she hadn't really seen Stefan out there; it had been a dream. Stefan was still missing.

"You have to do nothing of the kind," said Robert, Aunt Judith's fiancé. Elena had scarcely noticed him standing off to one side until then. But his tone brooked no argument. "The police are looking for Stefan; you leave them to their job," he said.

"The police think he killed Mr Tanner. But he didn't. You know that, don't you?" As Aunt Judith pulled her sodden outer sweater off, Elena looked from one face to another for help, but they were all the same. "You *know* he didn't do it," she repeated, almost desperately.

There was a silence. "Elena," Meredith said at last, "no one wants to think he did. But— well, it looks bad, his running away like this."

"He didn't run away. He didn't! He *didn't*—"

"Elena, hush," said Aunt Judith. "Don't get yourself worked up. I think you must be getting sick. It was so cold out there, and you got only a few hours of sleep last night . . ." She laid a hand on Elena's cheek.

Suddenly it was all too much for Elena. Nobody believed her, not even her friends and family. At that moment, she felt surrounded by enemies.

"I'm not sick," she cried, pulling away. "And I'm not crazy, either – whatever you think. Stefan didn't run away and he didn't kill Mr Tanner, and I don't care if none of you believes me . . ." She stopped, choking. Aunt Judith was fussing around her, hurrying her upstairs, and she let herself be hurried.

But she wouldn't go to bed when Aunt Judith suggested she must be tired. Instead, once she had warmed up, she sat on the living room couch by the fireplace, with blankets heaped around her. The phone rang all afternoon, and she heard Aunt Judith talking to friends, neighbours, the school. She assured all of them that Elena was fine. The . . . the tragedy last night had unsettled her a bit, that was all, and she seemed a little feverish. But she'd be as good as new after a rest.

Meredith and Bonnie sat beside her. "Do you want to talk?" Meredith said in a low voice. Elena shook her head, staring into the fire. They were all against her. And Aunt Judith was wrong; she wasn't fine. She wouldn't be fine until Stefan was found.

Matt stopped by, snow dusting his blond hair and his dark-blue parka. As he entered the room, Elena looked up at him hopefully. Yesterday Matt had helped save Stefan, when the rest of the school had wanted to lynch him. But today he returned her hopeful look with one of sober regret, and the concern in his blue eyes was only for her.

The disappointment was unbearable. "What are you doing here?" Elena demanded. "Keeping your promise to 'take care of me'?"

There was a flicker of hurt in his eyes. But Matt's voice was level. "That's part of it, maybe. But I'd try to take care of you anyway, no matter what I promised. I've been worried about you. Listen, Elena—"

She was in no mood to listen to anyone. "Well, I'm just fine, thank you. Ask anybody here. So you can stop worrying. Besides, I don't see why you should keep a promise to a *murderer*."

Startled, Matt looked at Meredith and Bonnie. Then he shook his head helplessly. "You're not being fair."

Elena was in no mood to be fair either. "I told you, you can stop worrying about me, and about my business. I'm fine, thanks."

The implication was obvious. Matt turned to the door just as Aunt Judith appeared with sandwiches.

"Sorry, I've got to go," he muttered, hurrying to the door. He left without looking back.

Meredith and Bonnie and Aunt Judith and Robert tried to make conversation while they ate an early supper by the fire. Elena couldn't eat and wouldn't talk. The only one who wasn't miserable was Elena's little sister, Margaret. With four-year-old optimism, she cuddled up to Elena and offered her some of her Hallowe'en candy.

Elena hugged her sister hard, her face pressed into Margaret's white-blonde hair for a moment. If Stefan could have called her or got a message to her, he would have done it by now. Nothing in the world would have stopped him, unless he were badly hurt, or trapped somewhere, or . . .

She wouldn't let herself think about that last "or". Stefan was alive; he had to be alive. Damon was a liar.

But Stefan was in trouble, and she had to find him somehow. She worried about it all through the evening, desperately trying to come up with a plan. One thing was clear; she was on her own. She couldn't trust anyone.

It grew dark. Elena shifted on the couch and forced a yawn.

"I'm tired," she said quietly. "Maybe I am sick after all. I think I'll go to bed."

Meredith was looking at her keenly. "I was just thinking, Miss Gilbert," she said, turning to Aunt Judith, "that maybe Bonnie and I should stay the night. To keep Elena company."

"What a good idea," said Aunt Judith, pleased. "As long as your parents don't mind, I'd be glad to have you."

"It's a long drive back to Herron. I think I'll stay, too," Robert said. "I can just stretch out on the couch here." Aunt Judith protested that there were plenty of guest bedrooms upstairs, but Robert was adamant. The couch would do just fine for him, he said.

After looking once from the couch to the hall where the front door stood plainly in view, Elena sat stonily. They'd planned this between them, or at least they were all in on it now. They were making sure she didn't leave the house.

When she emerged from the bathroom a little while later, wrapped in her red silk kimono, she found Meredith and Bonnie sitting on her bed.

"Well, hello, Rosencrantz and Guildenstern," she said bitterly.

Bonnie, who had been looking depressed, now looked alarmed. She glanced at Meredith doubtfully.

"She knows who we are. She means she thinks we're spies for her aunt," Meredith interpreted.

"Elena, you should realise that isn't so. Can't you trust us at all?"

"I don't know. Can I?"

"Yes, because we're your *friends*." Before Elena could move, Meredith jumped off the bed and shut the door. Then she turned to face Elena. "Now, for once in your life, listen to me, you little idiot. It's true we don't know what to think about Stefan. But, don't you see, that's your own fault. Ever since you and he got together, you've been shutting us out. Things have been happening that you haven't told us about. At least you haven't told us the whole story. But in spite of that, in spite of everything, we still trust you. We still care about you. We're still behind you, Elena, and we want to help. And if you can't see that, then you *are* an idiot."

Slowly, Elena looked from Meredith's dark, intense face to Bonnie's pale one. Bonnie nodded.

"It's true," she said, blinking hard as if to keep back tears. "Even if you don't like us, we still like *you*."

Elena felt her own eyes fill and her stern expression crumple. Then Bonnie was off the bed, and they were all hugging, and Elena found she couldn't help the tears that slid down her face.

"I'm sorry if I haven't been talking to you," she said. "I know you don't understand, and I can't even explain why I can't tell you everything. I just *can't*. But there's one thing I can tell you." She stepped back, wiping her cheeks, and looked at them earnestly. "No matter how bad the evidence against Stefan looks, *he didn't kill Mr Tanner*. I know he didn't, because I

know who did. And it's the same person who attacked
Vickie, and the old man under the bridge. And—" She
stopped and thought a moment. "—and, oh, Bonnie, I
think he killed Yangtze, too."

"*Yangtze?*" Bonnie's eyes widened. "But why would
he want to kill a dog?"

"I don't know, but he was there that night, in your
house. And he was . . . angry. I'm sorry, Bonnie."

Bonnie shook her head dazedly. Meredith said,
"Why don't you tell the police?"

Elena's laugh was slightly hysterical. "I can't. It's
not something they can deal with. And that's another
thing I can't explain. You said you still trusted me;
well, you'll just have to trust me about that."

Bonnie and Meredith looked at each other, then
at the bedspread, where Elena's nervous fingers
were picking a thread out of the embroidery. Finally
Meredith said, "All right. What can we do to
help?"

"I don't know. Nothing, unless . . ." Elena stopped
and looked at Bonnie. "Unless," she said, in a changed
voice, "you can help me find Stefan."

Bonnie's brown eyes were genuinely bewildered.
"Me? But what can I do?" Then, at Meredith's
indrawn breath, she said, "Oh. *Oh.*"

"You knew where I was that day I went to the
cemetery," said Elena. "And you even predicted
Stefan's coming to school."

"I thought you didn't believe in all that psychic
stuff," said Bonnie weakly.

"I've learned a thing or two since then. Anyway,

I'm willing to believe *anything* if it'll help find Stefan. If there's any chance at all it will help."

Bonnie was hunching up, as if trying to make her already tiny form as small as possible. "Elena, you don't understand," she said wretchedly. "I'm not trained; it's not something I can control. And–and it's not a game, not any more. The more you use those powers, the more they use *you*. Eventually they can end up using you all the time, whether you want it or not. It's *dangerous*."

Elena got up and walked to the cherry wood dresser, looking down at it without seeing it. At last she turned.

"You're right; it's not a game. And I believe you about how dangerous it can be. But it's not a game for Stefan, either. Bonnie, I think he's out there, somewhere, terribly hurt. And there's nobody to help him; nobody's even looking for him, except his enemies. He may be dying right now. He . . . he may even be . . ." Her throat closed. She bowed her head over the dresser and made herself take a deep breath, trying to steady herself. When she looked up, she saw that Meredith was looking at Bonnie.

Bonnie straightened her shoulders, sitting up as tall as she could. Her chin lifted and her mouth set. And in her normally soft brown eyes, a grim light shone as they met Elena's.

"We need a candle," was all she said.

The match rasped and threw sparks in the darkness, and then the candle flame burned strong and bright.

It lent a golden glow to Bonnie's pale face as she bent over it.

"I'm going to need both of you to help me focus," she said. "Look into the flame, and think about Stefan. Picture him in your mind. No matter what happens, keep on looking at the flame. And whatever you do, don't say anything."

Elena nodded, and then the only sound in the room was soft breathing. The flame flickered and danced, throwing patterns of light over the three girls sitting cross-legged around it. Bonnie, eyes closed, was breathing deeply and slowly, like someone drifting into sleep.

Stefan, thought Elena, gazing into the flame, trying to pour all her will into the thought. She created him in her mind, using all her senses, conjuring him to her. The roughness of his woollen sweater under her cheek, the smell of his leather jacket, the strength of his arms around her. Oh, Stefan . . .

Bonnie's lashes fluttered and her breathing quickened, like a sleeper having a bad dream. Elena resolutely kept her eyes on the flame, but when Bonnie broke the silence a chill went up her spine.

At first it was just a moan, the sound of someone in pain. Then, as Bonnie tossed her head, breath coming in short bursts, it became words.

"Alone . . ." she said, and stopped. Elena's nails bit into her hand. "Alone . . . in the dark," said Bonnie. Her voice was distant and tortured.

There was another silence, and then Bonnie began to speak quickly.

"It's dark and cold. And I'm alone. There's something behind me . . . jagged and hard. Rocks. They used to hurt – but not now. I'm numb now, from the cold. So cold . . ." Bonnie twisted, as if trying to get away from something, and then she laughed, a dreadful laugh almost like a sob. "That's . . . funny. I never thought I'd want to see the sun so much. But it's always dark here. And cold. Water up to my neck, like ice. That's funny, too. Water everywhere – and me dying of thirst. So thirsty . . . hurts . . ."

Elena felt something tighten around her heart. Bonnie was inside Stefan's thoughts, and who knew what she might discover there? Stefan, tell us where you are, she thought desperately. Look around; tell me what you see.

"Thirsty. I need . . . life?" Bonnie's voice was doubtful, as if not sure how to translate some concept. "I'm weak. He said I'll always be the weak one. He's strong . . . a killer. But that's what I am, too. I killed Katherine; maybe I deserve to die. Why not just let go? . . ."

"No!" said Elena before she could stop herself. In that instant, she forgot everything but Stefan's pain. "Stefan—"

"Elena!" Meredith cried sharply at the same time. But Bonnie's head fell forward, the flow of words cut off. Horrified, Elena realised what she had done.

"Bonnie, are you all right? Can you find him again? I didn't mean to . . ."

Bonnie's head lifted. Her eyes were open now, but they looked at neither the candle nor Elena. They stared straight ahead, expressionless. When she spoke, her voice was distorted, and Elena's heart stopped. It wasn't Bonnie's voice, but it was a voice Elena recognised. She'd heard it coming from Bonnie's lips once before, in the graveyard.

"Elena," the voice said, "don't go to the bridge. It's Death, Elena. Your death is waiting there." Then Bonnie slumped forward.

Elena grabbed her shoulders and shook. "Bonnie!" she almost screamed. "Bonnie!"

"What . . . oh, don't. Let go." Bonnie's voice was weak and shaken, but it was her own. Still bent over, she put a hand to her forehead.

"Bonnie, are you all right?"

"I think so . . . yes. But it was so strange." Her tone sharpened and she looked up, blinking. "What was that, Elena, about being a killer?"

"You remember that?"

"I remember everything. I can't describe it; it was awful. But what did that *mean*?"

"Nothing," said Elena. "He's hallucinating, that's all."

Meredith broke in. "He? Then you really think she tuned in to Stefan?"

Elena nodded, her eyes sore and burning as she looked away. "Yes. I think that was Stefan. It had to be. And I think she even told us where he is. Under Wickery Bridge, in the water."

CHAPTER

3

Bonnie stared. "I don't remember anything about the bridge. It didn't feel like a bridge."

"But you said it yourself, at the end. I thought you remembered . . ." Elena's voice died away. "You don't remember that part," she said flatly. It was not a question.

"I remember being alone, somewhere cold and dark, and feeling weak . . . and thirsty. Or was it hungry? I don't know, but I needed . . . something. And I almost wanted to die. And then you woke me up."

Elena and Meredith exchanged a glance. "And after that," Elena said to Bonnie, "you said one more thing, in a strange voice. You said not to go near the bridge."

"She told *you* not to go near the bridge," Meredith

corrected. "You in particular, Elena. She said Death was waiting."

"I don't care what's waiting," said Elena. "If that's where Stefan is, that's where I'm going."

"Then that's where we're all going," said Meredith.

Elena hesitated. "I can't ask you to do that," she said slowly. "There might be danger – of a kind you don't know about. It might be best for me to go alone."

"Are you kidding?" Bonnie said, sticking her chin out. "We *love* danger. I want to be young and beautiful in my grave, remember?"

"Don't," said Elena quickly. "You were the one who said it wasn't a game."

"And not for Stefan, either," Meredith reminded them. "We're not doing him much good standing around here."

Elena was already shrugging out of her kimono, moving towards the closet. "We'd better all bundle up. Borrow anything you want to keep warm," she said.

When they were more or less dressed for the weather, Elena turned to the door. Then she stopped.

"Robert," she said. "There's no way we can get past him to the front door, even if he's asleep."

Simultaneously, the three of them turned to look at the window.

"Oh, wonderful," said Bonnie.

As they climbed out into the quince tree, Elena realised that it had stopped snowing. But the bite of the air on her cheek made her remember Damon's words. Winter is an unforgiving season, she thought, and shivered.

All the lights in the house were out, including those in the living room. Robert must have gone to sleep already. Even so, Elena held her breath as they crept past the darkened windows. Meredith's car was a little way down the street. At the last minute, Elena decided to get some rope, and she soundlessly opened the back door to the garage. There was a swift current in Drowning Creek, and wading would be dangerous.

The drive to the end of town was tense. As they passed the outskirts of the woods, Elena remembered the way the leaves had blown at her in the cemetery. Particularly oak leaves.

"Bonnie, do oak trees have any special significance? Did your grandmother ever say anything about them?"

"Well, they were sacred to the Druids. All trees were, but oak trees were the most sacred. They thought the spirit of the trees brought them power."

Elena digested that in silence. When they reached the bridge and got out of the car, she gave the oak trees on the right side of the road an uneasy glance. But the night was clear and strangely calm, and no breeze stirred the dry brown leaves left on the branches.

"Keep your eyes out for a crow," she said to Bonnie and Meredith.

"A crow?" Meredith said sharply. "Like the crow outside Bonnie's house the night Yangtze died?"

"The night Yangtze was killed. Yes." Elena approached the dark waters of Drowning Creek with a rapidly beating heart. Despite its name, it was not a creek, but a swiftly flowing river with banks of red native clay. Above it stood Wickery Bridge, a wooden structure built nearly a century ago. Once, it had been strong enough to support wagons; now it was just a footbridge that nobody used because it was so out of the way. It was a barren, lonely, unfriendly place, Elena thought. Here and there patches of snow lay on the ground.

Despite her brave words earlier, Bonnie was hanging back. "Remember the last time we went over this bridge?" she said.

Too well, Elena thought. The last time they had crossed it, they were being chased by . . . something . . . from the graveyard. Or someone, she thought.

"We're not going over it yet," she said. "First we've got to look under it on this side."

"Where the old man was found with his throat torn open," Meredith muttered, but she followed.

The car headlights illuminated only a small portion of the bank under the bridge. As Elena stepped out of the narrow wedge of light, she felt a sick thrill of foreboding. Death was waiting, the voice had said. Was Death down here?

Her feet slipped on the damp, scummy stones. All she could hear was the rushing of the water, and its hollow echo from the bridge above her head. And, though she strained her eyes, all she could see in the darkness was the raw riverbank and the wooden trestles of the bridge.

"Stefan?" she whispered, and she was almost glad

that the noise of the water drowned her out. She felt like a person calling "who's there?" to an empty house, yet afraid of what might answer.

"This isn't right," said Bonnie from behind her.

"What do you mean?"

Bonnie was looking around, shaking her head slightly, her body taut with concentration. "It just feels wrong. I don't – well, for one thing I didn't hear the river before. I couldn't hear anything at all, just dead silence."

Elena's heart dropped with dismay. Part of her knew that Bonnie was right, that Stefan wasn't in this wild and lonely place. But part of her was too scared to listen.

"We've got to make sure," she said through the constriction in her chest, and she moved farther into the darkness, feeling her way along because she couldn't see. But at last she had to admit that there was no sign that any person had recently been here. No sign of a dark head in the water, either. She wiped cold muddy hands on her jeans.

"We can check the other side of the bridge," said Meredith, and Elena nodded mechanically. But she didn't need to see Bonnie's expression to know what they'd find. This was the wrong place.

"Let's just get out of here," she said, climbing through vegetation towards the wedge of light beyond the bridge. Just as she reached it, Elena froze.

Bonnie gasped. "Oh, God—"

"Get back," hissed Meredith. "Up against the bank."

Clearly silhouetted against the car headlights above

was a black figure. Elena, staring with a wildly beating heart, could tell nothing about it except that it was male. The face was in darkness, but she had a terrible feeling.

It was moving towards them.

Ducking out of sight, Elena cowered back against the muddy riverbank under the bridge, pressing herself as flat as possible. She could feel Bonnie shaking behind her, and Meredith's fingers sank into her arm.

They could see nothing from here, but suddenly there was a heavy footfall on the bridge. Scarcely daring to breathe, they clung to one another, faces turned up. The heavy footsteps rang across the wooden planks, moving away from them.

Please let him keep going, thought Elena. Oh, please . . .

She sank her teeth into her lip, and then Bonnie whimpered softly, her icy hand clutching Elena's. The footsteps were coming back.

I should go out there, Elena thought. It's me he wants, not them. He said as much. I should go out there and face him, and maybe he'll let Bonnie and Meredith leave. But the fiery rage that had sustained her that morning was in ashes now. With all her strength of will, she could not make her hand let go of Bonnie's, could not tear herself away.

The footsteps sounded right above them. Then there was silence, followed by a slithering sound on the bank.

No, thought Elena, her body charged with fear. He

was coming down. Bonnie moaned and buried her head against Elena's shoulder, and Elena felt every muscle tense as she saw movement – feet, legs – appear out of the darkness. *No . . .*

"What are you *doing* down there?"

Elena's mind refused to process this information at first. It was still panicking, and she almost screamed as Matt took another step down the bank, peering under the bridge.

"Elena? What are you *doing*?" he said again.

Bonnie's head flew up. Meredith's breath exploded in relief. Elena herself felt as if her knees might give way.

"*Matt*," she said. It was all she could manage.

Bonnie was more vocal. "What do you think *you're* doing?" she said in rising tones. "Trying to give us a heart attack? What are you out here for at this time of night?"

Matt thrust a hand into his pocket, rattling change. As they emerged from under the bridge, he stared out over the river. "I followed you."

"You *what*?" said Elena.

Reluctantly, he swung to face her. "I followed you," he repeated, shoulders tense. "I figured you'd find a way to get around your aunt and go out again. So I sat in my car across the street and watched your house. Sure enough, you three came climbing out of the window. So I followed you here."

Elena didn't know what to say. She was angry, and of course, he had probably done it only to keep his promise to Stefan. But the thought of Matt sitting out there in his battered old Ford, probably freezing to death and without any supper . . . it gave her a strange pang she didn't want to dwell on.

He was looking out at the river again. She stepped closer to him and spoke quietly.

"I'm sorry, Matt," she said. "About the way I acted back at the house, and – and about—" She fumbled for a minute and then gave up. About everything, she thought hopelessly.

"Well, I'm sorry for scaring you just now." He turned back briskly to face her, as if that settled the matter. "Now could you please tell me what you think you're doing?"

"Bonnie thought Stefan might be here."

"Bonnie did *not*," said Bonnie. "Bonnie said right away that it was the wrong place. We're looking for somewhere quiet, no noises, and closed in. I felt . . . surrounded," she explained to Matt.

Matt looked back at her warily, as if she might bite. "Sure you did," he said.

"There were rocks around me, but not like these river rocks."

"Uh, no, of course they weren't." He looked sideways at Meredith, who took pity on him.

"Bonnie had a vision," she said.

Matt backed up a little, and Elena could see his profile in the headlights. From his expression, she could tell he didn't know whether to walk away or to round them all up and cart them to the nearest mental asylum.

"It's no joke," she said. "Bonnie's psychic, Matt. I

know I've always said I didn't believe in that sort of thing, but I've been wrong. You don't know how wrong. Tonight, she – she tuned in to Stefan somehow and got a glimpse of where he is."

Matt drew a long breath. "I see. OK . . ."

"Don't patronise me! I'm not stupid, Matt, and I'm telling you this is for real. She was there, with Stefan; she knew things only he would know. And she saw the place he's trapped in."

"Trapped," said Bonnie. "That's it. It was definitely nothing open like a river. But there was water, water up to my neck. *His* neck. And rock walls around, covered with thick moss. The water was ice cold and still, and it smelled bad."

"But what did you *see*?" Elena said.

"Nothing. It was like being blind. Somehow I knew that if there was even the faintest ray of light I would be able to see, but I couldn't. It was as black as a tomb."

"As a tomb . . ." Thin chills went through Elena. She thought about the ruined church on the hill above the graveyard. There was a tomb there, a tomb she thought had opened once.

"But a tomb wouldn't be that wet," Meredith was saying.

"No . . . but I don't get any sense of where it *could* be then," Bonnie said. "Stefan wasn't really in his right mind; he was so weak and hurt. And so thirsty—"

Elena opened her mouth to stop Bonnie from going on, but just then Matt broke in.

"I'll tell you what it sounds like to me," he said.

The three girls looked at him, standing slightly apart from their group like an eavesdropper. They had almost forgotten about him.

"Well?" said Elena.

"Exactly," he said. "I mean, it sounds like a well."

Elena blinked, excitement stirring in her. "Bonnie?"

"It *could* be," said Bonnie slowly. "The size and the walls and everything would be right. But a well is open; I should have been able to see the stars."

"Not if it were covered," said Matt. "A lot of the old farmhouses around here have wells that are no longer in use, and some farmers cover them to make sure little kids don't fall in. My grandparents do."

Elena couldn't contain her excitement any longer. "That could be it. That *must* be it. Bonnie, remember, you said it was *always* dark there."

"Yes, and it did have a sort of underground feeling." Bonnie was excited, too, but Meredith interrupted with a dry question.

"How many wells do you think there are in Fell's Church, Matt?"

"Dozens, probably," he said. "But covered? Not as many. And if you're suggesting somebody dumped Stefan in this one, then it can't be any place where people would see it. Probably somewhere abandoned . . ."

"And his car was found on this road," said Elena.

"The old Francher place," said Matt.

They all looked at one another. The Francher farmhouse had been ruined and deserted for as long as anybody could remember. It stood in the middle of the woods, and the woods had taken it over nearly a century ago.

"Let's go," added Matt simply.

Elena put a hand on his arm. "You believe—?"

He looked away for a moment. "I don't know what to believe," he said at last. "But I'm coming."

They split up and took both cars, Matt with Bonnie in the lead, and Meredith following with Elena. Matt took a disused little cart track into the woods until it petered out.

"From here we walk," he said.

Elena was glad she'd thought of bringing rope; they'd need it if Stefan were really in the Francher well. And if he wasn't . . .

She wouldn't let herself think about that.

It was hard going through the woods, especially in the dark. The underbrush was thick, and dead branches reached out to snatch at them. Moths fluttered around them, brushing Elena's cheek with unseen wings.

Eventually they came to a clearing. The foundations of the old house could be seen, building stones tied to the ground now by weeds and brambles. For the most part, the chimney was still intact, with hollow places where concrete had once held it together, like a crumbling monument.

"The well would be somewhere out the back," Matt said.

It was Meredith who found it and called the others. They gathered around and looked at the flat, square block of stone almost level with the ground.

Matt stooped and examined the dirt and weeds around it. "It's been moved recently," he said.

That was when Elena's heart began pounding in earnest. She could feel it reverberating in her throat and her fingertips. "Let's get it off," she said in a voice barely above a whisper.

The stone slab was so heavy that Matt couldn't even shift it. Finally all four of them pushed, bracing themselves against the ground behind it, until, with a groan, the block moved a fraction of an inch. Once there was a tiny gap between stone and well, Matt used a dead branch to lever the opening wider. Then they all pushed again.

When there was an aperture large enough for her head and shoulders, Elena bent down, looking in. She was almost afraid to hope.

"Stefan?"

The seconds afterwards, hovering over that black opening, looking down into darkness, hearing only the echoes of pebbles disturbed by her movement, were agonising. Then, incredibly, there was another sound.

"Who—? Elena?"

"Oh, Stefan!" Relief made her wild. "Yes! I'm here, we're here, and we're going to get you out. Are you all right? Are you hurt?" The only thing that stopped her from tumbling in herself was Matt grabbing her from behind. "Stefan, hang on, we've got a rope. Tell me you're all right."

There was a faint, almost unrecognisable sound, but Elena knew what it was. A laugh. Stefan's voice was faint but intelligible. "I've – been better," he said. "But I'm – alive. Who's with you?"

"It's me. Matt," said Matt, releasing Elena. He bent over the hole himself. Elena, nearly delirious with elation, noted that he wore a slightly dazed look. "And Meredith and Bonnie, who's going to bend some spoons for us next. I'm going to throw you down a rope . . . that is, unless Bonnie can levitate you out." Still on his knees, he turned to look at Bonnie.

She slapped the top of his head. "Don't joke about it! Get him up!"

"Yes, ma'am," said Matt, a little giddily. "Here, Stefan. You're going to have to tie this around you."

"Yes," said Stefan. He didn't argue about fingers numb with cold or whether or not they could haul his weight up. There was no other way.

The next fifteen minutes were awful for Elena. It took all four of them to pull Stefan out, although Bonnie's main contribution was saying, "come on, come *on*," whenever they paused for breath. But at last Stefan's hands gripped the edge of the dark hole, and Matt reached forwards to grab him under the arms.

Then Elena was holding him, her arms locked around his chest. She could tell just how wrong things were by his unnatural stillness, by the limpness of his body. He'd used the last of his strength helping to pull himself out; his hands were cut and bloody. But what worried Elena most was the fact that those hands did not return her desperate embrace.

When she released him enough to look at him, she

saw that his skin was waxen, and there were black shadows under his eyes. His skin was so cold that it frightened her.

She looked up at the others anxiously.

Matt's brow was furrowed with concern. "We'd better get him to the clinic fast. He needs a doctor."

"No!" The voice was weak and hoarse, and it came from the limp figure Elena cradled. She felt Stefan gather himself, felt him slowly raise his head. His green eyes fixed on hers, and she saw the urgency in them.

"No . . . doctors." Those eyes burned into hers. "Promise . . . Elena."

Elena's own eyes stung and her vision blurred. "I promise," she whispered. Then she felt whatever had been holding him up, the current of sheer willpower and determination, collapse. He slumped in her arms, unconscious.

CHAPTER

"But he's got to have a doctor. He looks like he's dying!" said Bonnie.

"He can't. I can't explain right now. Let's just get him home, all right? He's wet and freezing out here. Then we can discuss it."

The job of getting Stefan through the woods was enough to occupy everyone's mind for a while. He remained unconscious, and when they finally laid him out in the back seat of Matt's car they were all bruised and exhausted, in addition to being wet from the contact with his soaking clothes. Elena held his head in her lap as they drove to the boarding house. Meredith and Bonnie followed.

"I see lights on," Matt said, parking in front of the large rust-red building. "She must be awake. But the door's probably locked."

Elena gently eased Stefan's head down and slipped out of the car, and saw one of the windows in the house brighten as a curtain was pushed aside. Then she saw a head and shoulders appear at the window, looking down.

"Mrs Flowers!" she called, waving. "It's Elena Gilbert, Mrs Flowers. We've found Stefan, and we need to get in!"

The figure at the window did not move or otherwise acknowledge her words. Yet from its posture, Elena could tell it was still looking down on them.

"Mrs Flowers, we have Stefan," she called again, gesturing to the lighted interior of the car. "Please!"

"Elena! It's unlocked already!" Bonnie's voice floated to her from the front porch, distracting Elena from the figure at the window. When she looked back up, she saw the curtains falling into place, and then the light in that upstairs room snapped off.

It was strange, but she had no time to puzzle over it. She and Meredith helped Matt lift Stefan and carry him up the front steps.

Inside, the house was dark and still. Elena directed the others up the staircase that stood opposite the door, and on to the second-floor landing. From there they went into a bedroom, and Elena had Bonnie open the door of what looked like a closet. It revealed another stairway, very dim and narrow.

"Who would leave their – front door unlocked – after all that's happened recently?" Matt grunted as they hauled their lifeless burden. "She must be crazy."

"She *is* crazy," Bonnie said from above, pushing the

door at the top of the staircase open. "Last time we were here she talked about the weirdest—" Her voice broke off in a gasp.

"What is it?" said Elena. But as they reached the threshold of Stefan's room, she saw for herself.

She'd forgotten the condition the room had been in the last time she'd seen it. Trunks filled with clothing were upended or lying on their sides, as if they'd been thrown by some giant hand from wall to wall. Their contents were strewn about the floor, along with articles from the dresser and tables. Furniture was overturned, and a window was broken, allowing a cold wind to blow in. There was only one lamp on, in a corner, and grotesque shadows loomed against the ceiling.

"*What happened?*" said Matt.

Elena didn't answer until they had stretched Stefan out on the bed. "I don't know for certain," she said, and this was true, if just barely. "But it was already this way last night. Matt, will you help me? He needs to get dry."

"I'll find another lamp," said Meredith, but Elena spoke quickly.

"No, we can see all right. Why don't you try to get a fire going?"

Spilling from one of the gaping trunks was a terry cloth robe of some dark colour. Elena took it, and she and Matt began to strip off Stefan's wet and clinging clothes. She worked on getting his sweater off, but one glimpse of his neck was enough to freeze her in place.

"Matt, could you – could you hand me that towel?"

As soon as he turned, she tugged the sweater over Stefan's head and quickly wrapped the robe around him. When Matt turned back and handed her the towel, she wound it around Stefan's throat like a scarf. Her pulse was racing, her mind working furiously.

No wonder he was so weak, so lifeless. Oh, God. She had to examine him, to see how bad it was. But how could she, with Matt and the others here?

"I'm going to get a doctor," Matt said in a tight voice, his eyes on Stefan's face. "He needs help, Elena."

Elena panicked. "Matt, no . . . please. He – he's afraid of doctors. I don't know what would happen if you brought one here." Again, it was the truth, if not the whole truth. She had an idea of what might help Stefan, but she couldn't do it with the others there. She bent over Stefan, rubbing his hands between her own, trying to think.

What could she do? Protect Stefan's secret at the cost of his life? Or betray him in order to save him? *Would* it save him to tell Matt and Bonnie and Meredith? She looked at her friends, trying to picture their response if they were to learn the truth about Stefan Salvatore.

It was no good. She couldn't risk it. The shock and horror of the discovery had nearly sent Elena herself reeling into madness. If she, who loved Stefan, had been ready to run from him screaming, what would these three do? And then there was Mr Tanner's murder. If they knew what Stefan was, would they ever be able to believe him innocent? Or, in their heart of hearts, would they always suspect him?

Elena shut her eyes. It was just too dangerous. Meredith and Bonnie and Matt were her friends, but this was one thing she couldn't share with them. In all the world, there was no one she could trust with this secret. She would have to keep it alone.

She straightened up and looked at Matt. "He's afraid of doctors, but a nurse might be all right." She turned to where Bonnie and Meredith were kneeling before the fireplace. "Bonnie, what about your sister?"

"Mary?" Bonnie glanced at her watch. "She has the late shift at the clinic this week, but she's probably home by now. Only—"

"Then that's it. Matt, you go with Bonnie and ask Mary to come here and look at Stefan. If she thinks he needs a doctor, I won't argue any more."

Matt hesitated, then exhaled sharply. "All right. I still think you're wrong, but – let's go, Bonnie. We're going to break some traffic laws."

As they went to the door, Meredith remained standing by the fireplace, watching Elena with steady dark eyes.

Elena made herself meet them. "Meredith . . . I think you should all go."

"Do you?" Those dark eyes remained on hers unwaveringly, as if trying to pierce through and read her mind. But Meredith did not ask any other questions. After a moment she nodded, and followed Matt and Bonnie without a word.

When Elena heard the door at the bottom of the

staircase close, she hastily righted a lamp that lay overturned by the bedside and plugged it in. Now, at last, she could take stock of Stefan's injuries.

His colour seemed worse than before; he was literally almost as white as the sheets below him. His lips were white, too, and Elena suddenly thought of Thomas Fell, the founder of Fell's Church. Or, rather, of Thomas Fell's statue, lying beside his wife's on the stone lid of their tomb. Stefan was the colour of that marble.

The cuts and gashes on his hands showed livid purple, but they were no longer bleeding. She gently turned his head to look at his neck.

And there it was. She touched the side of her own neck automatically, as if to verify the resemblance. But Stefan's marks were not small punctures. They were deep, savage tears in the flesh. He looked as if he had been mauled by some animal that had tried to rip out his throat.

White-hot anger blazed through Elena again. And with it, hatred. She realised that despite her disgust and fury, she had not really hated Damon before. Not really. But now . . . now, she *hated*. She loathed him with an intensity of emotion that she had never felt for anyone else in her life. She wanted to hurt him, to make him pay. If she'd had a wooden stake at that moment, she would have hammered it through Damon's heart without regret.

But just now she had to think of Stefan. He was so terrifyingly still. That was the hardest thing to bear, the lack of purpose or resistance in his body, the emptiness. That was it. It was as if he had vacated this form and left her with an empty vessel.

"Stefan!" Shaking him did nothing. With one hand on the centre of his cold chest, she tried to detect a heartbeat. If there was one, it was too faint to feel.

Keep calm, Elena, she told herself, pushing back the part of her mind that wanted to panic. The part that was saying, "What if he's dead? What if he's really dead, and nothing you can do will save him?"

Glancing about the room, she saw the broken window. Shards of glass lay on the floor beneath it. She went over and picked one up, noting how it sparkled in the firelight. A pretty thing, with an edge like a razor, she thought. Then, deliberately, setting her teeth, she cut her finger with it.

The pain made her gasp. After an instant, blood began welling out of the cut, dripping down her finger like wax down a candlestick. Quickly, she knelt by Stefan and put her finger to his lips.

With her other hand, she clasped his unresponsive one, feeling the hardness of the silver ring he wore. Motionless as a statue herself, she knelt there and waited.

She almost missed the first tiny flicker of response. Her eyes were fixed on his face, and she caught the minute lifting of his chest only in her peripheral vision. But then the lips beneath her finger quivered and parted slightly, and he swallowed reflexively.

"That's it," Elena whispered. "Come on, Stefan."

His eyelashes fluttered, and with dawning joy she

felt his fingers return the pressure of hers. He swallowed again.

"Yes." She waited until his eyes blinked and slowly opened before sitting back. Then she fumbled one-handed with the high neck of her sweater, folding it out of the way.

Those green eyes were dazed and heavy, but as stubborn as she had ever seen them. "No," Stefan said, his voice a cracked whisper.

"You have to, Stefan. The others are coming back and bringing a nurse with them. I had to agree to that. And if you're not well enough to convince her you don't need a hospital . . ." She left the sentence unfinished. She herself didn't know what a doctor or lab technician would find examining Stefan. But she knew he knew, and that it made him afraid.

But Stefan only looked more obstinate, turning his face away from her. "Can't," he whispered. "It's too dangerous. Already took . . . too much . . . last night."

Could it have been only last night? It seemed a year ago. "Will it kill me?" she asked. "Stefan, answer me! Will it kill me?"

"No . . . " His voice was sullen. "But—"

"Then we have to do it. Don't argue with me!" Bending over him, holding his hand in hers, Elena could feel his overpowering need. She was amazed that he was even trying to resist. It was like a starving man standing before a banquet, unable to take his eyes from the steaming dishes, but refusing to eat.

"No," Stefan said again, and Elena felt frustration surge through her. He was the only person she'd ever met who was as stubborn as she was.

"*Yes*. And if you won't cooperate I'll cut something else, like my wrist." She had been pressing her finger into the sheet to staunch the blood; now she held it up to him.

His pupils dilated, his lips parted. "Too much . . . already," he murmured, but his gaze remained on her finger, on the bright drop of blood at the tip. "And I can't . . . control . . ."

"It's all right," she whispered. She drew the finger across his lips again, feeling them open to take it in; then, she leaned over him and shut her eyes.

His mouth was cool and dry as it touched her throat. His hand cupped the back of her neck as his lips sought the two little punctures already there. Elena willed herself not to recoil at the brief sting of pain. Then she smiled.

Before, she had felt his agonising need, his driving hunger. Now, through the bond they shared, she felt only fierce joy and satisfaction. Deep satisfaction as the hunger was gradually assuaged.

Her own pleasure came from giving, from knowing that she was sustaining Stefan with her own life. She could sense the strength flowing into him.

In time, she felt the intensity of the need lessen. Still, it was by no means gone, and she could not understand when Stefan tried to push her away.

"That's enough," he grated, forcing her shoulders up. Elena opened her eyes, her dreamy pleasure broken. His own eyes were green as mandrake leaves, and in his face she saw the fierce hunger of the predator.

"It isn't enough. You're still weak—"

"It's enough for *you*." He pushed at her again, and she saw something like desperation spark in those green eyes. "Elena, if I take much more, you will begin to change. And if you don't move away, if you don't move away from me *right now* . . ."

Elena withdrew to the foot of the bed. She watched him sit up and adjust the dark robe. In the lamplight, she saw that his skin had regained some colour, a slight flush glazing its pallor. His hair was drying into a tumbled sea of dark waves.

"I missed you," she said softly. Relief throbbed within her suddenly, an ache that was almost as bad as the fear and tension had been. Stefan was alive; he was talking to her. Everything was going to be all right after all.

"Elena . . ." Their eyes met and she was held by green fire. Unconsciously, she moved towards him, and then stopped as he laughed aloud.

"I've never seen you look like this before," he said, and she looked down at herself. Her shoes and jeans were caked with red mud, which was also liberally smeared over the rest of her. Her jacket was torn and leaking its down stuffing. She had no doubt that her face was smudged and dirty, and she *knew* her hair was tangled and straggly. Elena Gilbert, immaculate fashion plate of Robert E Lee, was a mess.

"I like it," Stefan said, and this time she laughed with him.

They were still laughing as the door opened. Elena stiffened alertly, twitching at her turtleneck, glancing around the room for evidence that might betray them. Stefan sat up straighter and licked his lips.

"He's better!" Bonnie caroled out as she stepped into the room and saw Stefan. Matt and Meredith were right behind her, and their faces lit with surprise and pleasure. The fourth person who came in was only a little older than Bonnie, but she had an air of brisk authority that belied her youth. Mary McCullough went straight over to her patient and reached for his pulse.

"So you're the one afraid of doctors," she said.

Stefan looked disconcerted for a moment; then, he recovered. "It's sort of a childhood phobia," he said, sounding embarrassed. He glanced sideways at Elena, who smiled nervously and gave a tiny nod. "Anyway, I don't need one now, as you can see."

"Why don't you let me be the judge of that? Your pulse is all right. In fact, it's surprisingly slow, even for an athlete. I don't think you're hypothermic, but you're still chilled. Let's get a temperature."

"No, I really don't think that's necessary." Stefan's voice was low, calming. Elena had heard him use that voice before, and she knew what he was trying to do. But Mary took not the slightest notice.

"Open up, please."

"Here, I'll do it," said Elena quickly, reaching to take the thermometer from Mary. Somehow, as she did so, the little glass tube slipped out of her hand. It fell to the hardwood floor and smashed into several pieces. "Oh, I'm sorry!"

"It doesn't matter," Stefan said. "I'm feeling much better than I was, and I'm getting warmer all the time."

Mary regarded the mess on the floor, then looked around the room, taking in its ransacked state. "All right," she demanded, turning around with hands on hips. "What's been going on here?"

Stefan didn't even blink. "Nothing much. Mrs Flowers is just a terrible housekeeper," he said, looking her straight in the eye.

Elena wanted to laugh, and she saw that Mary did, too. The older girl grimaced and crossed her arms over her chest instead. "I suppose it's useless to hope for a straight answer," she said. "And it's clear you're not dangerously ill. I can't *make* you go to the clinic. But I'd strongly suggest you get a check-up tomorrow."

"Thank you," said Stefan, which, Elena noticed, was not the same as agreeing.

"Elena, *you* look as if you could use a doctor," said Bonnie. "You're white as a ghost."

"I'm just tired," Elena said. "It's been a long day."

"My advice is to go home and go to bed – and stay there," Mary said. "You're not anaemic, are you?"

Elena resisted the impulse to put a hand to her cheek. Was she so pale? "No, I'm just tired," she repeated. "We can go home now, if Stefan's all right."

He nodded reassuringly, the message in his eyes for her alone. "Give us a minute, will you?" he said to

Mary and the others, and they stepped back to the staircase.

"Goodbye. Take care of yourself," Elena said aloud as she hugged him. She whispered, "Why didn't you use your Powers on Mary?"

"I did," he said grimly in her ear. "Or at least I tried. I must still be weak. Don't worry; it'll pass."

"Of course, it will," said Elena, but her stomach lurched. "Are you sure you should be alone, though? What if—"

"I'll be fine. You're the one who shouldn't be alone." Stefan's voice was soft but urgent. "Elena, I didn't get a chance to warn you. You were right about Damon being in Fell's Church."

"I know. *He* did this to you, didn't he?" Elena didn't mention that she'd gone searching for him.

"I – don't remember. But he's dangerous. Keep Bonnie and Meredith with you tonight, Elena. I don't want you alone. And make sure no one invites a stranger into your house."

"We're going straight to bed," Elena promised, smiling at him. "We won't be inviting anybody in."

"Make sure of it." There was no flippancy in his tone at all, and she nodded slowly.

"I understand, Stefan. We'll be careful."

"Good." They kissed, a mere brushing of lips, but their joined hands separated only reluctantly. "Tell the others 'thank you'," he said.

"I will."

The five of them regrouped outside the boarding house, Matt offering to drive Mary home so Bonnie and Meredith could go back with Elena. Mary was still clearly suspicious about the night's goings-on, and Elena couldn't blame her. She also couldn't think. She was too tired.

"He said to say 'thanks' to all of you," she remembered after Matt had left.

"He's . . . welcome," Bonnie said, splitting the words with an enormous yawn as Meredith opened the car door for her.

Meredith said nothing. She had been very quiet since leaving Elena alone with Stefan.

Bonnie laughed suddenly. "One thing we all forgot about," she said. "The prophecy."

"What prophecy?" said Elena.

"About the bridge. The one you say I said. Well, you went to the bridge and Death wasn't waiting there after all. Maybe you misunderstood the words."

"No," said Meredith. "We heard the words correctly all right."

"Well, then, maybe it's another bridge. Or . . . mmm . . ." Bonnie snuggled down in her coat, shutting her eyes, and didn't bother to finish.

But Elena's mind completed the sentence for her. *Or another time.*

An owl hooted outside as Meredith started the car.

CHAPTER

2 November, Saturday
Dear Diary,

This morning I woke up and felt so strange. I don't know how to describe it. On the one hand, I was so weak that when I tried to stand up my muscles wouldn't support me. But on the other hand I felt . . . pleasant. So comfortable, so relaxed. As if I were floating on a bed of golden light. I didn't care if I never moved again.

Then I remembered Stefan, and I tried to get up, but Aunt Judith put me back to bed. She said Bonnie and Meredith had left hours ago, and that I'd been so fast asleep they couldn't wake me. She said what I needed was rest.

So here I am. Aunt Judith brought the TV in, but I don't care about watching it. I'd rather lie here and write, or just lie here.

I'm expecting Stefan to call. He told me he would. Or

maybe he didn't. I can't remember. When he does call I have to

3 November, Sunday (10:30 pm)

I've just read over yesterday's entry and I'm shocked. What was wrong with me? I broke off in the middle of a sentence, and now I don't even know what I was going to say. And I didn't explain about my new diary or anything. I must have been completely spaced out.

Anyway, this is the official start of my new diary. I bought this blank book at the chemist. It's not as beautiful as the other one, but it will have to do. I've given up hope of ever seeing my old one again. Whoever stole it isn't going to bring it back. But when I think of them reading it, all my inner thoughts and my feelings about Stefan, I want to kill them. While simultaneously dying of humiliation myself.

I'm not ashamed of the way I feel about Stefan. But it's private. And there are things in there, about the way it is when we kiss, when he holds me, that I know he wouldn't want anybody else to read.

Of course, it hasn't got anything about his secret in it. I hadn't found that out yet. It wasn't until I did that I really understood him, and we got together, really together, at last. Now we're part of each other. I feel as if I've been waiting for him all my life.

Maybe you think I'm terrible for loving him, considering what he is. He can be violent, and I know there are some things in his past that he's ashamed of. But he could never be violent towards me, and the past is over. He has so much guilt and he hurts so much inside. I want to heal him.

I don't know what will happen now; I'm just so glad that

he's safe. I went to the boarding house today and found out that the police had been there yesterday. Stefan was still weak and couldn't use his Powers to get rid of them, but they didn't accuse him of anything. They just asked questions. Stefan says they acted friendly, which makes me suspicious. What all the questions really boil down to is: where were you on the night the old man was attacked under the bridge, and the night Vickie Bennett was attacked in the ruined church, and the night Mr Tanner was killed at school?

They don't have any evidence against him. So the crimes started right after he came to Fell's Church, so what? That's not proof of anything. So he argued with Mr Tanner that night. Again, so what? Everybody argued with Mr Tanner. So he disappeared after Mr Tanner's body was found. He's back now, and it's pretty clear that he was attacked himself, by the same person who committed the other crimes. Mary told the police about the condition he was in. And if they ever ask us, Matt and Bonnie and Meredith and I can all testify how we found him. There's no case against him at all.

Stefan and I talked about that, and about other things. It was so good to be with him again, even if he did look white and tired. He still doesn't remember how Thursday night ended, but most of it is just as I suspected. Stefan went to find Damon on Thursday night after he took me home. They argued. Stefan ended up half-dead in a well. It doesn't take a genius to figure out what happened in between.

I still haven't told him that I went looking for Damon in the graveyard Friday morning. I suppose I'd better do it tomorrow. I know he's going to be upset, especially when he hears what Damon said to me.

Well, that's all. I'm tired. This diary is going to be well-hidden, for obvious reasons.

Elena paused and looked at the last line on the page. Then she added:

P.S. I wonder who our new European history teacher will be?

She tucked the diary under her mattress and turned out the light.

Elena walked down the hallway in a curious vacuum. At school she was usually peppered with greetings from all sides; it was "hi, Elena" after "hi, Elena" wherever she went. But today eyes slid away furtively as she approached, or people suddenly became very busy doing something that required them to keep their backs to her. It had been happening all day long.

She paused in the doorway of the European History classroom. There were several students already sitting down, and at the chalkboard was a stranger.

He looked almost like a student himself. He had sandy hair, worn a little long, and the build of an athlete. Across the board he had written "Alaric K Saltzman." As he turned around, Elena saw that he also had a boyish smile.

He went on smiling as Elena sat down and other students filed in. Stefan was among them, and his eyes met Elena's as he took his seat beside her, but they didn't speak. No one was talking. The room was dead silent.

Bonnie sat down on Elena's other side. Matt was only a few desks away, but he was looking straight ahead.

The last two people to come in were Caroline Forbes and Tyler Smallwood. They walked in together, and Elena didn't like the look on Caroline's face. She knew that catlike smile and those narrowed green eyes all too well. Tyler's handsome, rather fleshy features were shining with satisfaction. The discolouration under his eyes caused by Stefan's fist was almost gone.

"OK, to start off, why don't we put all these desks in a circle?"

Elena's attention snapped back to the stranger at the front of the room. He was still smiling.

"Come on, let's do it. That way we can all see each other's faces when we talk," he said.

Silently, the students obeyed. The stranger didn't sit at Mr Tanner's desk; instead, he pulled a chair to the circle and straddled it backwards.

"Now," he said. "I know you all must be curious about me. My name's on the board: Alaric K Saltzman. But I want you to call me Alaric. I'll tell you a little more about me later, but first I want to give *you* a chance to talk.

"Today's probably a difficult day for most of you. Someone you cared about is gone, and that must hurt. I want to give you a chance to open up and share those feelings with me and with your classmates. I want you to try to get in touch with the pain. Then we can start to build our own relationship on trust. Now who would like to go first?"

They stared at him. No one so much as moved an eyelash.

"Well, let's see . . . what about you?" Still smiling, he gestured encouragingly to a pretty, fair-haired girl. "Tell us your name and how you feel about what's happened."

Flustered, the girl stood. "My name's Sue Carson, and, uh . . ." She took a deep breath and went doggedly on. "And I feel *scared*. Because whoever this maniac is, he's still loose. And next time it could be me." She sat down.

"Thank you, Sue. I'm sure a lot of your classmates share your concern. Now, do I understand that some of you were actually there when this tragedy occurred?"

Desks creaked as students shifted uneasily. But Tyler Smallwood stood up, his lips drawing back from strong white teeth in a smile.

"*Most* of us were there," he said, and his eyes flickered toward Stefan. Elena could see other people following his gaze. "I got there right after Bonnie discovered the body. And what I feel is concern for the community. There's a dangerous killer on the streets, and so far nobody's done anything to stop him. And—" He broke off. Elena wasn't sure how, but she felt Caroline had signalled him to do it. Caroline tossed back gleaming auburn hair and recrossed her long legs as Tyler took his seat again.

"OK, thank you. So most of you were there. That

makes it doubly hard. Can we hear from the person who actually found the body? Is Bonnie here?" He looked around.

Bonnie raised her hand slowly, then stood. "I *guess* I discovered the body," she said. "I mean, I was the first person who knew that he was really dead, and not just faking."

Alaric Saltzman looked slightly startled. "Not just faking? Did he often fake being dead?" There were titters, and he flashed that boyish smile again. Elena turned and glanced at Stefan, who was frowning.

"No – no," said Bonnie. "You see, he was a sacrifice. At the Haunted House. So he was covered with blood anyway, only it was fake blood. And that was partly my fault, because he didn't want to put it on, and I told him he had to do it. He was supposed to be a Bloody Corpse. But he kept saying it was too messy, and it wasn't until Stefan came and argued with him—" She stopped. "I mean, we talked to him and he finally agreed to do it, and then the Haunted House started. And a little while later I noticed that he wasn't sitting up and scaring the kids like he was supposed to, and I went over and asked him what was wrong. And he didn't answer. He just – he just kept staring at the ceiling. And then I touched him and he – it was terrible. His head just sort of *flopped* . . ." Bonnie's voice wavered and gave out. She gulped.

Elena was standing up, and so were Stefan and Matt and a few other people. Elena reached over to Bonnie.

"Bonnie, it's OK. Bonnie, don't. It's OK."

"And blood got all over my hands. There was blood everywhere, so much blood . . ." She sniffed hysterically.

"OK, time out," Alaric Saltzman said. "I'm sorry; I didn't mean to distress you so much. But I think you need to work through these feelings sometime in the future. It's clear that this has been a pretty devastating experience."

He stood up and paced around the centre of the circle, his hands opening and shutting nervously. Bonnie was still sniffling softly.

"I know," he said, the boyish smile coming back in full force. "I'd like to get our student-teacher relationship off to a good start, away from this whole atmosphere. How about if you all come around to my place this evening, and we can all talk informally? Maybe just get to know each other, maybe talk about what happened. You can even bring a friend if you want. How about it?"

There was another thirty seconds or so of staring. Then someone said, "Your place?"

"Yes . . . oh, I'm forgetting. Stupid of me. I'm staying at the Ramsey house, on Magnolia Avenue." He wrote the address on the board. "The Ramseys are friends of mine, and they loaned me the house while they're on holiday. I come from Charlottesville, and your principal called me on Friday to ask me if I could take over here. I jumped at the chance. This is my first real teaching job."

"Oh, that explains it," said Elena under her breath.

"Does it?" said Stefan.

"Anyway, what do you think? Is it a plan?" Alaric Saltzman looked around at them.

No one had the heart to refuse. There were scattered "yeses" and "sures."

"Great, then it's settled. I'll provide the refreshments, and we'll all get to know each other. Oh, by the way . . ." He opened a grade book and scanned it. "In this class, participation makes up half your final grade." He glanced up and smiled. "You can go now."

"The nerve of him," somebody muttered as Elena went out the door. Bonnie was behind her, but Alaric Saltzman's voice called her back.

"Would the students who shared with us please stay behind for a minute?"

Stefan had to leave, too. "I'd better go check about football practice," he said. "It's probably cancelled, but I'd better make sure."

Elena was concerned. "If it's not cancelled, do you think you're feeling up to it?"

"I'll be fine," he said evasively. But she noticed that his face still looked drawn, and he moved as if he were in pain. "Meet you at your locker," he said.

She nodded. When she got to her locker, she saw Caroline nearby talking to two other girls. Three pairs of eyes followed Elena's every move as she put away her books, but when Elena glanced up, two of them suddenly looked away. Only Caroline remained staring at her, head slightly cocked as she whispered something to the other girls.

Elena had had enough. Slamming her locker, she

walked straight towards the group. "Hello, Becky; hello, Sheila," she said. Then, with heavy emphasis: "Hello, Caroline."

Becky and Sheila mumbled "hello" and added something about having to leave. Elena didn't even turn to watch them slink away. She kept her eyes on Caroline's.

"What's going on?" she demanded.

"Going on?" Caroline was obviously enjoying this, trying to draw it out as long as possible. "Going on with who?"

"With you, Caroline. With everybody. Don't pretend you're not up to something, because I know you are. People have been avoiding me all day as if I had the plague, and you look like you've just won the lottery. What have you done?"

Caroline's expression of innocent inquiry slipped, and she smiled a feline smile. "I told you when school started that things were going to be different this year, Elena," she said. "I warned you that your time on the throne might be running out. But it isn't *my* doing. What's happening is simply natural selection. The law of the jungle."

"And just what *is* happening?"

"Well, let's just say that going out with a murderer can put the dampers on your social life."

Elena's chest tightened as if Caroline had hit her. For a moment, the desire to hit Caroline back was almost irresistible. Then, with the blood pounding in her ears, she said through clenched teeth, "That isn't true. Stefan hasn't done anything. The police questioned him, and he was cleared."

Caroline shrugged. Her smile now was patronising. "Elena, I've known you since kindergarten," she said, "so I'll give you some advice for old times' sake: drop Stefan. If you do it right now you might just avoid being a complete social leper. Otherwise you might as well buy yourself a little bell to ring in the street."

Rage held Elena hostage as Caroline turned and walked away, her auburn hair moving like liquid under the lights. Then Elena found her tongue.

"Caroline." The other girl turned back. "Are you going to go to that party at the Ramsey house tonight?"

"I suppose so. Why?"

"Because I'll be there. With Stefan. See you in the jungle." This time Elena was the one to turn away.

The dignity of her exit was slightly marred when she saw a slim, shadowed figure at the far end of the hallway. Her step faltered for an instant, but as she drew closer she recognised Stefan.

She knew the smile she gave him looked forced, and he glanced back towards the lockers as they walked side by side out of the school.

"So football practice was cancelled?" she said.

He nodded. "What was that all about?" he said quietly.

"Nothing. I asked Caroline if she was going to the party tonight." Elena tilted back her head to look at the grey and dismal sky.

"And that's what you were talking about?"

She remembered what he had told her in his room.

He could see better than a human, and hear better, too. Well enough to catch words spoken down forty feet of corridor?

"Yes," she said defiantly, still inspecting the clouds.

"And that's what made you so angry?"

"Yes," she said again, in the same tone.

She could feel his eyes on her. "Elena, that's not true."

"Well, if you can read my mind, you don't need to ask me questions, do you?"

They were facing each other now. Stefan was tense, his mouth set in a grim line. "You know I wouldn't do that. But I thought you were the one who was so big on honesty in relationships."

"All right. Caroline was being her usual bitchy self and shooting her mouth off about the murder. So what? Why do you care?"

"Because," said Stefan simply, brutally, "she might be right. Not about the murder but about you. About you and me. I should have realised this would happen. It's not just her, is it? I've been sensing hostility and fear all day, but I was too tired to try and analyse it. They think I'm the killer and they're taking it out on you."

"What they think doesn't matter! They're wrong, and they'll realise that eventually. Then everything will be the way it was again."

A wistful smile tugged at the corner of Stefan's mouth. "You really believe that, don't you?" He looked away, and his face hardened. "And what if they don't? What if it only gets worse?"

"What are you saying?"

"It might be better . . ." Stefan took a deep breath and continued, carefully. "It might be better if we didn't see each other for a while. If they think we're not together, they'll leave you alone."

She stared at him. "And you think you could do that? Not see me or talk to me for however long?"

"If it's necessary – yes. We could pretend we've broken up." His jaw was set.

Elena stared for another moment. Then she circled him and moved in closer, so close that they were almost touching. He had to look down at her, his eyes only a few inches from her own.

"There is," she said, "only one way I'm going to announce to the rest of the school that we've broken up. And that's if you tell me that you don't love me and you don't want to see me. Tell me that, Stefan, right now. Tell me that you don't want to be with me any more."

He'd stopped breathing. He stared down at her, those green eyes patterned like a cat's in shades of emerald and malachite and holly green.

"Say it," she told him. "Tell me how you can get along without me, Stefan. Tell me—"

She never got to finish the sentence. It was cut off as his mouth descended on hers.

CHAPTER

6

Stefan sat in the Gilbert living room, agreeing politely with whatever it was Aunt Judith was saying. The older woman was uncomfortable having him here; you didn't need to be a mind reader to know that. But she was trying, and so Stefan was trying, too. He wanted Elena to be happy.

Elena. Even when he wasn't looking at her, he was aware of her more than of anything else in the room. Her living presence beat against his skin like sunlight against closed eyelids. When he actually let himself turn to face her, it was a sweet shock to all his senses.

He loved her so much. He never saw her as Katherine any more; he had almost forgotten how much she looked like the dead girl. In any case, there were so many differences. Elena had the same pale

63

gold hair and creamy skin, the same delicate features as Katherine, but there the resemblance ended. Her eyes, looking violet in the firelight just now but normally a blue as dark as lapis lazuli, were neither timid nor childlike as Katherine's had been. On the contrary, they were windows to her soul, which shone like an eager flame behind them. Elena was Elena, and her image had replaced Katherine's gentle ghost in his heart.

But her very strength made their love dangerous. He hadn't been able to resist her last week when she'd offered him her blood. Granted, he might have died without it, but it had been far too soon for Elena's own safety. For the hundredth time, his eyes moved over Elena's face, searching for the telltale signs of change. Was that creamy skin a little paler? Was her expression slightly more remote?

They would have to be careful from now on. *He* would have to be more careful. Make sure to feed often, satisfy himself with animals, so he wouldn't be tempted. Never let the need get too strong. Now that he thought of it, he was hungry right now. The dry ache, the burning, was spreading along his upper jaw, whispering through his veins and capillaries. He should be out in the woods – senses alert to catch the slightest crackle of dry twigs, muscles ready for the chase – not here by a fire watching the tracery of pale blue veins in Elena's throat.

That slim throat turned as Elena looked at him.

"Do you want to go to that party tonight? We can take Aunt Judith's car," she said.

"But you ought to stay for dinner first," said Aunt Judith quickly.

"We can pick up something on the way." Elena meant they could pick up something for her, Stefan thought. He himself could chew and swallow ordinary food if he had to, though it did him no good, and he had long since lost any taste for it. No, his . . . appetites . . . were more particular now, he thought. And if they went to this party, it would mean hours more before he could feed. But he nodded agreement to Elena.

"If you want to," he said.

She did want to; she was set on it. He'd seen that from the beginning. "All right then, I'd better change."

He followed her to the base of the stairway. "Wear something with a high neck. A sweater," he told her in a voice too low to carry.

She glanced through the doorway, to the empty living room, and said, "It's all right. They're almost healed already. See?" She tugged her lacy collar down, twisting her head to one side.

Stefan stared, mesmerised, at the two round marks on the fine-grained skin. They were a very light, translucent burgundy colour, like much-watered wine. He set his teeth and forced his eyes away. Looking much longer at that would drive him crazy.

"That wasn't what I meant," he said brusquely.

The shining veil of her hair fell over the marks again, hiding them. "Oh."

* * *

"Come in!"

As they did, walking into the room, conversations stopped. Elena looked at the faces turned towards them, at the curious, furtive eyes and the wary expressions. Not the kind of looks she was used to getting when she made an entrance.

It was another student who'd opened the door for them; Alaric Saltzman was nowhere in sight. But Caroline was, seated on a bar stool, which showed off her legs to their best advantage. She gave Elena a mocking look and then made some remark to a boy on her right. He laughed.

Elena could feel her smile start to go painful, while a flush crept up towards her face. Then a familiar voice came to her.

"Elena, Stefan! Over here."

Gratefully, she spotted Bonnie sitting with Meredith and Ed Goff on a loveseat in the corner. She and Stefan settled on a large ottoman opposite them, and she heard conversations start to pick up again around the room.

By tacit agreement, no one mentioned the awkwardness of Elena and Stefan's arrival. Elena was determined to pretend that everything was as usual.

And Bonnie and Meredith were backing her. "You look great," said Bonnie warmly. "I just love that red sweater."

"She does look nice. Doesn't she, Ed?" said Meredith, and Ed, looking vaguely startled, agreed.

"So your class was invited to this, too," Elena said

to Meredith. "I thought maybe it was just seventh period."

"I don't know if *invited* is the word," replied Meredith dryly. "Considering that participation is half our grade."

"Do you think he was serious about that? He couldn't be serious," put in Ed.

Elena shrugged. "He sounded serious to me. Where's Ray?" she asked Bonnie.

"Ray? Oh, Ray. I don't know, around somewhere, I suppose. There's a lot of people here."

That was true. The Ramsey living room was packed, and from what Elena could see the crowd flowed into the dining room, the front parlour, and probably the kitchen as well. Elbows kept brushing Elena's hair as people circulated behind her.

"What did Saltzman want with you after class?" Stefan was saying.

"Alaric," Bonnie corrected primly. "He wants us to call him Alaric. Oh, he was just being nice. He felt awful for making me relive such an agonising experience. He didn't know exactly how Mr Tanner died, and he hadn't realised I was so sensitive. Of course, he's incredibly sensitive himself, so he understands what it's like. He's an Aquarius."

"With a moon rising in pick-up lines," said Meredith under her breath. "Bonnie, you don't believe that garbage, do you? He's a teacher; he shouldn't be trying that out on students."

"He wasn't trying anything out! He said exactly the same thing to Tyler and Sue Carson. He said we should form a support group for each other or write an essay about that night to get our feelings out. He said teenagers are all very impressionable and he didn't want the tragedy to have a lasting impact on our lives."

"Oh, brother," said Ed, and Stefan turned a laugh into a cough. He wasn't amused, though, and his question to Bonnie hadn't been just idle curiosity. Elena could tell; she could feel it radiating from him. Stefan felt about Alaric Saltzman the way that most of the people in this room felt about Stefan. Wary and mistrustful.

"It *was* strange, him acting as if the party was a spontaneous idea in our class," she said, responding unconsciously to Stefan's unspoken words, "when obviously it had been planned."

"What's even stranger is the idea that the school would hire a teacher without telling him how the previous teacher died," said Stefan. "Everyone was talking about it; it must have been in the papers."

"But not all the details," said Bonnie firmly. "In fact, there are things the police still haven't let out, because they think it might help them catch the killer. For instance," she dropped her voice, "do you know what Mary said? Dr Feinberg was talking to the guy who did the autopsy, the medical examiner. And he said that there was no blood left in the body at all. Not a drop."

Elena felt an icy wind blow through her, as if she stood once again in the graveyard. She couldn't speak. But Ed said, "Where'd it go?"

"Well, all over the floor, I suppose," said Bonnie calmly. "All over the altar and everything. That's what the police are investigating now. But it's unusual for a corpse not to have *any* blood left; usually there's some that settles down on the underside of the body. Postmortem lividity, it's called. It looks like big purple bruises. What's wrong?"

"Your incredible sensitivity has me ready to throw up," said Meredith in a strangled voice. "Could we possibly talk about something else?"

"*You* weren't the one with blood all over you," Bonnie began, but Stefan interrupted her.

"Have the investigators come to any conclusions from what they've learned? Are they any closer to finding the killer?"

"I don't know," said Bonnie, and then she brightened. "That's right, Elena, you said you knew—"

"Shut up, Bonnie," said Elena desperately. If there ever were a place *not* to discuss that, it was in a crowded room surrounded by people who hated Stefan. Bonnie's eyes widened, and then she nodded, subsiding.

Elena could not relax, though. Stefan hadn't killed Mr Tanner, and yet the same evidence that would lead to Damon could as easily lead to him. And *would* lead to him, because no one but she and Stefan knew of Damon's existence. He was out there, somewhere, in the shadows. Waiting for his next victim. Maybe waiting for Stefan – or for her.

"I'm hot," she said abruptly. "I think I'll go and see what kinds of refreshments *Alaric* has provided."

Stefan started to rise, but Elena waved him back down. He wouldn't have any use for potato chips and punch. And she wanted to be alone for a few minutes, to be moving instead of sitting, to calm herself.

Being with Meredith and Bonnie had given her a false sense of security. Leaving them, she was once again confronted by sidelong glances and suddenly turned backs. This time it made her angry. She moved through the crowd with deliberate insolence, holding any eye she accidentally caught. I'm already notorious, she thought. I might as well be brazen, too.

She was hungry. In the Ramsey dining room someone had set up an assortment of finger foods that looked surprisingly good. Elena took a paper plate and dropped a few carrot sticks on it, ignoring the people around the bleached oak table. She wasn't going to speak to them unless they spoke first. She gave her full attention to the refreshments, leaning past people to select cheese wedges and Ritz crackers, reaching in front of them to pluck grapes, ostentatiously looking up and down the whole array to see if there was anything she'd missed.

She'd succeeded in riveting everyone's attention, something she knew without raising her eyes. She bit delicately down on a bread stick, holding it between her teeth like a pencil, and turned from the table.

"Mind if I have a bite?"

Shock snapped her eyes wide open and froze her breath. Her mind jammed, refusing to acknowledge what was going on, and leaving her helpless, vulnerable, in the face of it. But though rational thought had disappeared, her senses went right on recording mercilessly: dark eyes dominating her field of vision, a whiff of some kind of cologne in her nostrils, two long fingers tilting her chin up. Damon leaned in, and, neatly and precisely, bit off the other end of the bread stick.

In that moment, their lips were only inches apart. He was leaning in for a second bite before Elena's wits revived enough to throw her backward, her hand grabbing the bit of crisp bread and tossing it away. He caught it in midair, a virtuoso display of reflex.

His eyes were still on hers. Elena got in a breath at last and opened her mouth; she wasn't sure what for. To scream, probably. To warn all these people to run out into the night. Her heart was pounding like a hammer, her vision blurred.

"Easy, easy." He took the plate from her and then somehow got hold of her wrist. He was holding it lightly, the way Mary had felt for Stefan's pulse. As she continued to stare and gasp, he stroked it with his thumb, as if comforting her. "Easy. It's all right."

What are you doing here? she thought. The scene around her seemed eerily bright and unnatural. It was like one of those nightmares when everything is ordinary, just like waking life, and then suddenly something grotesque happens. He was going to kill them all.

"Elena? Are you OK?" Sue Carson was talking to her, gripping her shoulder.

"I think she choked on something," Damon said,

releasing Elena's wrist. "But she's all right now. Why don't you introduce us?"

He was going to kill them all . . .

"Elena, this is Damon, um . . ." Sue spread an apologetic hand, and Damon finished for her.

"Smith." He lifted a paper cup toward Elena. "*La vita.*"

"What are you doing here?" she whispered.

"He's a college student," Sue volunteered, when it became apparent that Damon wasn't going to answer. "From – University of Virginia, was it? William and Mary?"

"Among other places," Damon said, still looking at Elena. He hadn't glanced at Sue once. "I like to travel."

The world had snapped into place again around Elena, but it was a chilling world. There were people on every side, watching this exchange with fascination, keeping her from speaking freely. But they were also keeping her safe. For whatever reason, Damon was playing a game, pretending to be one of them. And while the masquerade went on, he wouldn't do anything to her in front of a crowd . . . she hoped.

A game. But he was making up the rules. He was standing here in the Ramseys' dining room playing with her.

"He's just down for a few days," Sue was continuing helpfully. "Visiting – friends, did you say? Or relatives?"

"Yes," said Damon.

"You're lucky to be able to take off whenever you want," Elena said. She didn't know what was possessing her, to make her try and unmask him.

"Luck has very little to do with it," said Damon. "Do you like dancing?"

"What's your major?"

He smiled at her. "American folklore. Did you know, for instance, that a mole on the neck means you'll be wealthy? Do you mind if I check?"

"*I* mind." The voice came from behind Elena. It was clear and cold and quiet. Elena had heard Stefan speak in that tone only once: when he had found Tyler trying to assault her in the graveyard. Damon's fingers stilled on her throat, and, released from his spell, she stepped back.

"But do you matter?" he said.

The two of them faced each other under the faintly flickering yellow light of the brass chandelier.

Elena was aware of layers of her own thoughts, like a parfait. Everyone's staring; this must be better than the movies . . . I didn't realise Stefan was taller . . . There's Bonnie and Meredith wondering what's going on . . . Stefan's angry but he's still weak, still hurting . . . If he goes for Damon now, he'll lose . . .

And in front of all these people. Her thoughts came to a clattering halt as everything fell into place. That was what Damon was here for, to make Stefan attack him, apparently unprovoked. No matter what happened after that, he won. If Stefan drove him away, it would just be more proof of Stefan's "tendency toward violence". More evidence for Stefan's accusers. And if Stefan lost the fight . . .

It would mean his life, thought Elena. Oh, Stefan,

he's so much stronger right now; please don't do it. Don't play into his hands. He *wants* to kill you; he's just looking for a chance.

She made her limbs move, though they were stiff and awkward as a marionette's. "Stefan," she said, taking his cold hand in hers, "let's go home."

She could feel the tension in his body, like an electric current running underneath his skin. At this moment, he was completely focused on Damon, and the light in his eyes was like fire reflecting off a dagger blade. She didn't recognise him in this mood, didn't know him. He frightened her.

"*Stefan*," she said, calling to him as if she were lost in fog and couldn't find him. "Stefan, *please*."

And slowly, slowly, she felt him respond. She heard him breathe and felt his body go off alert, clicking down to some lower energy level. The deadly concentration of his mind was diverted and he looked at her, and saw her.

"All right," he said softly, looking into her eyes. "Let's go."

She kept her hands on him as they turned away, one clasping his hand, the other tucked inside his arm. By sheer force of will, she managed not to look over her shoulder as they walked away, but the skin on her back tingled and crawled as if expecting the stab of a knife.

Instead, she heard Damon's low ironic voice: "And have you heard that kissing a red-haired girl cures fever blisters?" And then Bonnie's outrageous, flattered laughter.

On the way out, they finally ran into their host.

"Leaving so soon?" Alaric said. "But I haven't even had a chance to talk to you yet."

He looked both eager and reproachful, like a dog that knows perfectly well it's *not* going to be taken on a walk but wags anyway. Elena felt worry blossom in her stomach for him and everyone else in the house. She and Stefan were leaving them to Damon.

She'd just have to hope her earlier assessment was right and he wanted to continue the masquerade. Right now she had enough to do getting Stefan out of here before he changed his mind.

"I'm not feeling very well," she said as she picked up her purse where it lay by the ottoman. "Sorry." She increased the pressure on Stefan's arm. It would take very little to get him to turn back and head for the dining room right now.

"*I'm* sorry," said Alaric. "Goodbye."

They were on the threshold before she saw the little slip of violet paper stuck into the side pocket of her purse. She pulled it out and unfolded it almost by reflex, her mind on other things.

There was writing on it, plain and bold and unfamiliar. Just three lines. She read them and felt the world rock. This was too much; she couldn't deal with anything more.

"What is it?" said Stefan.

"Nothing." She thrust the bit of paper back into the side pocket, pushing it down with her fingers. "It's nothing, Stefan. Let's get outside."

They stepped out into driving needles of rain.

CHAPTER

7

"**N**ext time," Stefan said quietly, "I won't leave."

Elena knew he meant it, and it terrified her. But just now her emotions were quietly coasting in neutral, and she didn't want to argue.

"He was there," she said. "Inside an ordinary house full of ordinary people, just as if he had every right to be. I wouldn't have thought he would dare."

"Why not?" Stefan said briefly, bitterly. "*I* was there in a ordinary house full of ordinary people, just as if I had every right to be."

"I didn't mean that the way it sounded. It's just that the only other time I've seen him in public was at the Haunted House when he was wearing a mask and costume, and it was dark. Before that it was always somewhere deserted, like the gym that night I was there alone, or the graveyard . . ."

She knew as soon as she said that last part that it was a mistake. She still hadn't told Stefan about going to find Damon three days ago. In the driver's seat, he stiffened.

"Or the graveyard?"

"Yes . . . I meant that day Bonnie and Meredith and I got chased out. I'm assuming it must have been Damon who chased us. And the place was deserted except for the three of us."

Why was she lying to him? Because, a small voice in her head answered grimly, otherwise he might snap. Knowing what Damon had said to her, what he had promised was in store, might be all that was needed to send Stefan over the edge.

I can never tell him, she realised with a sick jolt. Not about that time or about anything Damon does in the future. If he fights Damon, he dies.

Then he'll never know, she promised herself. No matter what I have to do, I'll keep them from fighting each other over me. No matter what.

For a moment, apprehension chilled her. Five hundred years ago, Katherine had tried to keep them from fighting, and had succeeded only in forcing them into a death match. But *she* wouldn't make the same mistake, Elena told herself fiercely. Katherine's methods had been stupid and childish. Who else but a stupid child would kill herself in the hope that the two rivals for her hand would become friends? It had been the worst mistake of the whole sorry affair. Because of it, the rivalry between Stefan and Damon had turned into implacable hatred. And what's more,

Stefan had lived with the guilt of it ever since; he blamed himself for Katherine's stupidity and weakness.

Groping for another subject, she said, "Do you think someone invited him in?"

"Obviously, since he *was* in."

"Then it's true about – people like you. You have to be invited in. But Damon got into the gym without an invitation."

"That's because the gym isn't a dwelling place for the living. That's the one criterion. It doesn't matter if it's a house or a tent or an apartment above a store. If living humans eat and sleep there, we need to be invited inside."

"But I didn't invite you into *my* house."

"Yes, you did. That first night, when I drove you home, you pushed the door open and nodded to me. It doesn't have to be a verbal invitation. If the intent is there, that's enough. And the person inviting you doesn't have to be someone who actually lives in the house. Any human will do."

Elena was thinking. "What about a houseboat?"

"Same thing. Although running water can be a barrier in itself. For some of us, it's almost impossible to cross."

Elena had a sudden vision of herself and Meredith and Bonnie racing for Wickery Bridge. Because somehow she had known that if they got to the other side of the river they'd be safe from whatever was after them.

"So *that's* why," she whispered. It still didn't explain

how she'd known, though. It was as if the knowledge had been put into her head from some outside source. Then she realised something else.

"You took me across the bridge. You can cross running water."

"That's because I'm weak." It was said flatly, with no emotion behind it. "It's ironic, but the stronger your Powers are, the more you're affected by certain limitations. The more you belong to the dark, the more the rules of the dark bind you."

"What other rules are there?" said Elena. She was beginning to see the glimmer of a plan. Or at least of the hope of a plan.

Stefan looked at her. "Yes," he said, "I think it's time you knew. The more you know about Damon, the more chance you'll have of protecting yourself."

Of protecting herself? Perhaps Stefan knew more than she thought. But as he turned the car on to a side street and parked, she just said, "OK. Should I be stocking up on garlic?"

He laughed. "Only if you want to be unpopular. There are certain plants, though, that might help you. Like vervain. That's a herb that's supposed to protect you against bewitchment, and it can keep your mind clear even if someone is using Powers against you. People used to wear it around their necks. Bonnie would love it; it was sacred to the Druids."

"Vervain," said Elena, tasting the unfamiliar word. "What else?"

"Strong light, or direct sunlight, can be very painful. You'll notice the weather's changed."

"I've noticed," said Elena after a beat. "You mean Damon's doing that?"

"He must be. It takes enormous power to control the elements, but it makes it easy for him to travel in daylight. As long as he keeps it cloudy, he doesn't even need to protect his eyes."

"And neither do you," Elena said. "What about – well, crosses and things?"

"No effect," said Stefan. "Except that if the person holding one *believes* it's a protection, it can strengthen their will to resist tremendously."

"Uh . . . silver bullets?"

Stefan laughed again shortly. "That's for werewolves. From what I've heard they don't like silver in any form. A wooden stake through the heart is still the approved method for my kind. There are other ways that are more or less effective, though: burning, beheading, driving nails through the temples. Or, best of all—"

"Stefan!" The lonely, bitter smile on his face dismayed her. "What about changing into animals?" she said. "Before, you said that with enough Power you could do that. If Damon can be any animal he likes, how will we ever recognise him?"

"Not any animal he likes. He's limited to one animal, or at the most two. Even with his Powers I don't think he could sustain any more than that."

"So we keep looking out for a crow."

"Right. You may be able to tell if he's around, too, by looking at regular animals. They usually don't react very well to us; they sense that we're hunters."

"Yangtze kept barking at that crow. It was as if he knew there was something wrong about it," Elena remembered. "Ah . . . Stefan," she added in a changed tone as a new thought struck her, "what about mirrors? I don't remember ever seeing you in one."

For a moment, he didn't answer. Then he said, "Legend has it that mirrors reflect the soul of the person who looks into them. That's why primitive people are afraid of mirrors; they're afraid that their souls will be trapped and stolen. My kind is supposed to have no reflection – because we have no souls." Slowly, he reached up to the rearview mirror and tilted it downwards, adjusting it so that Elena could look into it. In the silvered glass, she saw his eyes, lost, haunted, and infinitely sad.

There was nothing to do but hold on to him, and Elena did. "I love you," she whispered. It was the only comfort she could give him. It was all they had.

His arms tightened around her; his face was buried in her hair. "You're the mirror," he whispered back.

It was good to feel him relax, tension flowing out of his body as warmth and comfort flowed in. She was comforted, too, a sense of peace infusing her, surrounding her. It was so good that she forgot to ask him what he meant until they were at her front door, saying goodbye.

"I'm the mirror?" she said then, looking up at him.

"You've stolen my soul," he said. "Lock the door behind you, and don't open it again tonight." Then he was gone.

* * *

"Elena, thank heavens," said Aunt Judith. When Elena stared at her, she added, "Bonnie called from the party. She said you'd left unexpectedly, and when you didn't come home I was worried."

"Stefan and I went for a ride." Elena didn't like the expression on her aunt's face when she said that. "Is there a problem?"

"No, no. It's just . . ." Aunt Judith didn't seem to know how to finish her sentence. "Elena, I wonder if it might be a good idea to . . . not see quite so much of Stefan."

Elena went still. "You, too?"

"It isn't that I believe the gossip," Aunt Judith assured her. "But, for your own sake, it might be best to get a little distance from him, to—"

"To dump him? To abandon him because people are spreading rumours about him? To keep myself away from the mud slinging in case any of it sticks on me?" Anger was a welcome release, and the words crowded in Elena's throat, all trying to get out at once. "No, I *don't* think that's a good idea, Aunt Judith. And if it were Robert we were talking about, you wouldn't either. Or maybe you would!"

"Elena, I will not have you speaking to me in that tone—"

"I'm finished anyway!" Elena cried, and whirled blindly for the stairs. She managed to keep the tears back until she was in her own room with the door locked. Then she threw herself on the bed and sobbed.

* * *

She dragged herself up a while later to call Bonnie. Bonnie was excited and talkative. What on earth did Elena mean, had anything unusual happened after she and Stefan left? The unusual thing was their leaving! No, that new guy Damon hadn't said anything about Stefan afterwards; he'd just hung around for a while and then disappeared. No, Bonnie hadn't seen if he left with anybody. Why? Was Elena jealous? Yes, that was meant to be a joke. But, really, he *was* gorgeous, wasn't he? Almost more gorgeous than Stefan, that is assuming you liked dark hair and eyes. Of course, if you liked lighter hair and hazel eyes . . .

Elena immediately deduced that Alaric Saltzman's eyes were hazel.

She got off the phone at last and only then remembered the note she'd found in her purse. She should have asked Bonnie if anyone had gone near her purse while she was in the dining room. But then, Bonnie and Meredith had been in the dining room part of the time themselves. Someone might have done it then.

The very sight of the violet paper made her taste tin at the back of her mouth. She could hardly bear to look at it. But now that she was alone she *had* to unfold it and read it again, all the time hoping that somehow this time the words might be different, that she might have been mistaken before.

But they weren't different. The sharp, clean letters stood out against the pale background as if they were ten feet high.

I want to touch him. More than any boy I've ever known. And I know he wants it, too, but he's holding back on me.

Her words. From her diary. The one that had been stolen.

The next day Meredith and Bonnie rang her doorbell.

"Stefan called me last night," said Meredith. "He said he wanted to make sure you weren't walking to school alone. He's not going to be at school today, so he asked if Bonnie and I could come over and walk with you."

"Escort you," said Bonnie, who was clearly in a good mood. "Chaperone you. I think it's terribly sweet of him to be so protective."

"He's probably an Aquarius, too," said Meredith. "Come on, Elena, before I kill her to shut her up about Alaric."

Elena walked in silence, wondering what Stefan was doing that kept him from school. She felt vulnerable and exposed today, as if her skin were on inside out. One of those days when she was ready to cry at the drop of a hat.

On the office bulletin board was tacked a piece of violet paper.

She should have known. She *had* known somewhere deep inside. The thief wasn't satisfied with letting her know her private words had been read. He was showing her they could be made public.

She ripped the note off the board and crumpled it, but not before she glimpsed the words. In one glance they were seared on to her brain.

I feel as if someone has hurt him terribly in the past and he's never got over it. But I also think there's something he's afraid of, some secret he's afraid I'll find out.

"Elena, what is that? What's the matter? Elena, come back here!"

Bonnie and Meredith followed her to the nearest girls' bathroom, where she stood over the wastebasket shredding the note into microscopic pieces, breathing as if she'd just run a race. They looked at each other and then turned to survey the bathroom stalls.

"OK," said Meredith loudly, "senior privilege. You!" She rapped on the only closed door. "Come out."

Some rustling, then a bewildered freshman emerged. "But I didn't even—"

"Out. Outside," Bonnie ordered. "And *you*," she said to the girl washing her hands, "stand out there and make sure nobody comes in."

"But why? What are you—"

"*Move*. If anybody comes through that door we're holding you responsible."

When the door was closed again, they rounded on Elena.

"OK, this is a stick-up," said Meredith. "Come on, Elena, give."

Elena ripped the last tiny shred of paper, caught between laughter and tears. She wanted to tell them everything, but she couldn't. She settled for telling them about the diary.

They were as angry, as indignant, as she was.

"It had to be someone at the party," Meredith said at last, once they had each expressed their opinion of the thief's character, morals, and probable destination in the afterlife. "But anybody there could have done it. I don't remember anyone in particular going near your purse, but that room was wall-to-wall people, and it could have happened without my noticing."

"But why would anyone *want* to do this?" Bonnie put in. "Unless . . . Elena, the night we found Stefan you were hinting around at some things. You said you thought you knew who the killer was."

"I don't think I know; I *know*. But if you're wondering if this might be connected, I'm not sure. I suppose it could be. The same person might have done it."

Bonnie was horrified. "But that means the killer is a student at this school!" When Elena shook her head, she went on. "The only people at that party who weren't students were that new guy and Alaric." Her expression changed. "Alaric didn't kill Mr Tanner! He wasn't even in Fell's Church then."

"I know. Alaric didn't do it." She'd gone too far to stop now; Bonnie and Meredith already knew too much. "Damon did."

"That guy was the *killer*? The guy that *kissed* me?"

"Bonnie, calm down." As always, other people's hysteria made Elena feel more in control. "Yes, he's the killer, and we all three have to be on guard against him. That's why I'm telling you. Never, never ask him into your house."

Elena stopped, regarding the faces of her friends. They were staring at her, and for a moment she had the sickening feeling that they didn't believe her. That they were going to question her sanity.

But all Meredith asked, in an even, detached voice, was: "Are you sure about this?"

"Yes. I'm sure. He's the murderer and the one who put Stefan in the well, and he might be after one of us next. And I don't know if there's any way to stop him."

"Well, then," said Meredith, lifting her eyebrows. "No wonder you and Stefan were in such a hurry to leave the party."

Caroline gave Elena a vicious smirk as Elena walked into the cafeteria. But Elena was almost beyond noticing.

One thing she noticed right away, though. Vickie Bennett was there.

Vickie hadn't been to school since the night Matt and Bonnie and Meredith had found her wandering on the road, raving about mist and eyes and something terrible in the graveyard. The doctors who checked her afterwards said there was nothing much wrong with her physically, but she still hadn't returned to Robert E Lee. People whispered about psychologists and the drug treatments they were trying.

She didn't look crazy, though, Elena thought. She looked pale and subdued and sort of crumpled into her clothing. And when Elena passed her and she looked up, her eyes were like a startled fawn's.

It was strange to sit at a half-empty table with only Bonnie and Meredith for company. Usually people were crowding to get seats around the three of them.

"We didn't finish talking this morning," Meredith

said. "Get something to eat, and then we'll figure out what to do about those notes."

"I'm not hungry," said Elena flatly. "And what *can* we do? If it's Damon, there's no way we can stop him. Trust me, it's not a matter for the police. That's why I haven't told them he's the killer. There isn't any proof, and besides, they would never . . . Bonnie, you're not listening."

"Sorry," said Bonnie, who was staring past Elena's left ear. "But something weird is going on up there."

Elena turned. Vickie Bennett was standing at the front of the cafeteria, but she no longer seemed crumpled and subdued. She was looking around the room in a sly and assessing manner, smiling.

"Well, she doesn't look normal, but I wouldn't say she was being *weird*, exactly," Meredith said. Then she added, "Wait a minute."

Vickie was unbuttoning her cardigan. But it was the *way* she was doing it – with deliberate little flicks of her fingers, all the while looking around with that secretive smile – that was odd. When the last button was undone, she took the sweater daintily between forefinger and thumb and slid it down over first one arm and then the other. She dropped the sweater on the floor.

"Weird is the word," confirmed Meredith.

Students crossing in front of Vickie with laden trays glanced at her curiously and then looked back over their shoulders when they had passed. They didn't actually stop walking, though, until she took off her shoes.

She did it gracefully, catching the heel of one pump on the toe of the other and pushing it off. Then she kicked off the second pump.

"She can't keep going," murmured Bonnie, as Vickie's fingers moved to the simulated pearl buttons on her white silk blouse.

Heads were turning; people were poking one another and gesturing. Around Vickie a small group had gathered, standing far enough back that they didn't interfere with everyone else's view.

The white silk blouse rippled off, fluttering like a wounded ghost to the floor. Vickie was wearing a lacy off-white slip underneath.

There was no longer any sound in the cafeteria except the sibilance of whispers. No one was eating. The group around Vickie had got larger.

Vickie smiled demurely and began to unfasten clasps at her waist. Her pleated skirt fell to the floor. She stepped out of it and pushed it to one side with her foot.

Somebody stood up at the back of the cafeteria and chanted, "Take it *off*! Take it *off*!" Other voices joined in.

"Isn't anybody going to stop her?" fumed Bonnie.

Elena got up. The last time she'd gone near Vickie the other girl had screamed and struck out at her. But now, as she got close, Vickie gave her the smile of a conspirator. Her lips moved, but Elena couldn't make out what she was saying over the chanting.

"Come on, Vickie. Let's go," she said.

Vickie's light brown hair tossed and she plucked at the strap of her slip.

Elena stooped to pick up the cardigan and wrap it around the girl's slender shoulders. As she did, as she touched Vickie, those half-closed eyes opened wide like a startled fawn's again. Vickie stared about her wildly, as if she'd just been awakened from a dream. She looked down at herself and her expression turned to disbelief. Pulling the cardigan around her more tightly, she backed away, shivering.

The room was quiet again.

"It's OK," said Elena soothingly. "Come on."

At the sound of her voice, Vickie jumped as if touched by a live wire. She stared at Elena, and then she exploded into action.

"You're one of them! I saw you! You're evil!"

She turned and ran barefoot out of the cafeteria, leaving Elena stunned.

"**D**o you know what's strange about what Vickie did at school? I mean aside from all the obvious things," Bonnie said, licking chocolate frosting off her fingers.

"What?" said Elena dully.

"Well, the way she ended up, in her slip. She looked just like she did when we found her on the road, only then she was all scratched up, too."

"Cat scratches, we thought," said Meredith, finishing the last bite of her cake. She seemed to be in one of her quiet, thoughtful moods; right now she was watching Elena closely. "But that doesn't seem very likely."

Elena looked straight back at her. "Maybe she fell in some brambles," she said. "Now, if you guys are finished eating, do you want to see that first note?"

They left their dishes in the sink and climbed the

stairs to Elena's room. Elena felt herself flush as the other girls read the note. Bonnie and Meredith were her best friends, maybe her only friends now. She'd read them passages from her diary before. But this was different. It was the most humiliating feeling she'd ever had. "Well?" she said to Meredith.

"The person who wrote this is five feet eleven inches tall, walks with a slight limp, and wears a false moustache," Meredith intoned. "Sorry," she added, seeing Elena's face. "Not funny. Actually, there's not much to go on, is there? The writing looks like a guy's, but the paper looks feminine."

"And the whole thing has sort of a feminine touch," put in Bonnie, bouncing slightly on Elena's bed. "Well, it does," she said defensively. "Quoting bits of your diary back at you is the kind of thing a woman would think of. Men don't care about diaries."

"You just don't want it to be Damon," said Meredith. "I would think you'd be more worried about him being a psycho killer than a diary thief."

"I don't know; killers are sort of romantic. Imagine your dying with his hands around your throat. He'd strangle the life out of you, and the last thing you'd see would be his face." Putting her own hands to her throat, Bonnie gasped and expired tragically, ending up draped across the bed. "He can have me anytime," she said, eyes still closed.

It was on Elena's lips to say, "Don't you understand, this is *serious*," but instead she hissed in a breath. "Oh, *God*," she said, and ran to the window. The day was humid and stifling, and the window had been opened.

Outside on the skeletal branches of the quince tree was a crow.

Elena threw the sash down so hard that the glass rattled and tinkled. The crow gazed at her through the trembling panes with eyes like obsidian. Rainbows glimmered in its sleek black plumage.

"Why did you *say* that?" she said, turning to Bonnie.

"Hey, there's nobody out there," said Meredith gently. "Unless you count the birds."

Elena turned away from them. The tree was empty now.

"I'm sorry," said Bonnie in a small voice, after a moment. "It's just that it all doesn't seem real sometimes, even Mr Tanner's being dead doesn't seem real. And Damon did look . . . well, exciting. But dangerous. I can believe he's dangerous."

"And besides, he wouldn't squeeze your throat; he'd cut it," Meredith said. "Or at least that was what he did to Tanner. But the old man under the bridge had his throat ripped open, as if some animal had done it." Meredith looked to Elena for clarification. "Damon doesn't have an animal, does he?"

"No. I don't know." Suddenly, Elena felt very tired. She was worried about Bonnie, about the consequences of those foolish words.

"I can do anything to you, to you and the ones you love," she remembered. What might Damon do now? She didn't understand him. He was different every time they met. In the gym he'd been taunting, laughing at her. But the next time she would swear that he'd been serious, quoting poetry to her, trying to get her to come away with him. Last week, with the icy graveyard wind lashing around him, he'd been menacing, cruel. And underneath his mocking words last night, she'd felt the same menace. She couldn't predict what he'd do next.

But, whatever happened, she had to protect Bonnie and Meredith from him. Especially since she couldn't warn them properly.

And what was Stefan up to? She needed him right now, more than anything. Where *was* he?

It started that morning.

"Let me get this straight," Matt said, leaning against the scarred body of his ancient Ford sedan when Stefan approached him before school. "You want to borrow my car."

"Yes," Stefan said.

"And the reason you want to borrow it is flowers. You want to get some flowers for Elena."

"Yes."

"And these particular flowers, these flowers you've just got to get, don't grow around here."

"They might. But their blooming season is over this far north. And the frost would have finished them off anyway."

"So you want to go down south – how far south you don't know – to find some of these flowers that you've just got to give to Elena."

"Or at least some of the plants," Stefan said. "I'd rather have the actual flowers though."

"And since the police still have your car, you want

to borrow mine, for however long it takes you to go down south and find these flowers that you've just got to give to Elena."

"I figure driving is the least conspicuous way to leave town," Stefan explained. "I don't want the police to follow me."

"Uh huh. And that's why you want my car."

"Yes. Are you going to give it to me?"

"Am I going to give my car to the guy who stole my girlfriend and now wants to take a jaunt down south to get her some kind of special flowers she's just got to have? Are you crazy?" Matt, who had been staring out over the roofs of the frame houses across the street, turned at last to look at Stefan. His blue eyes, usually cheerful and straightforward, were full of utter disbelief, and surmounted by twisted, puckered brows.

Stefan looked away. He should have known better. After everything Matt had already done for him, to expect more was ridiculous. Especially these days, when people flinched from the sound of his step and avoided his eyes when he came near. To expect Matt, who had the best of reasons to resent him, to do him such a favour with no explanation, on the basis of faith alone, really *was* insane.

"No, I'm not crazy," he said quietly, and turned to go.

"Neither am I," Matt had said. "And I'd have to be crazy to turn my car over to you. Hell, no. I'm going with you."

By the time Stefan had turned back around, Matt was looking at the car instead of him, lower lip thrust forward in a wary, judicious pout.

"After all," he'd said, rubbing at the flaking vinyl of the roof, "you might scratch the paint or something."

Elena put the phone back on the hook. *Somebody* was at the boarding house, because somebody kept picking up the phone when it rang, but after that there was only silence and then the click of disconnection. She suspected it was Mrs Flowers, but that didn't tell her anything about where Stefan was. Instinctively, she wanted to go to him. But it was dark outside, and Stefan had warned her specifically not to go out in the dark, especially not anywhere near the cemetery or the woods. The boarding house was near both.

"No answer?" said Meredith as Elena came back and sat down on the bed.

"She keeps hanging up on me," Elena said, and muttered something under her breath.

"Did you say she was a witch?"

"No, but it rhymes with that," said Elena.

"Look," said Bonnie, sitting up. "If Stefan's going to call, he'll call here. There's no reason for you to come and stay the night with me."

There *was* a reason, although Elena couldn't quite explain it even to herself. After all, Damon had kissed Bonnie at Alaric Saltzman's party. It was Elena's fault that Bonnie was in danger in the first place. Somehow she felt that if she were at least on the scene, she might be able to protect Bonnie.

"My mum and dad and Mary are all home," Bonnie persisted. "And we lock all our doors and windows and everything since Mr Tanner was murdered. This weekend Dad even put on extra locks. I don't see what *you* can do."

Elena didn't either. But she was going just the same.

She left a message for Stefan with Aunt Judith, telling him where she was. There was still a lingering constraint between her and her aunt. And there would be, Elena thought, until Aunt Judith changed her mind about Stefan.

At Bonnie's house, she was given a room that had belonged to one of Bonnie's sisters who was now in college. The first thing she did was check the window. It was closed and locked, and there was nothing outside that someone could climb, like a drainpipe or tree. As inconspicuously as possible, she also checked Bonnie's room and any others she could get into. Bonnie was right; they were all sealed up tight from the inside. Nothing from the outside could get in.

She lay in bed a long time that night, staring at the ceiling, unable to sleep. She kept remembering Vickie dreamily doing a striptease in the cafeteria. What was wrong with the girl? She would remember to ask Stefan that next time she saw him.

Thoughts of Stefan were pleasant, even with all the terrible things that had happened recently. Elena smiled in the darkness, letting her mind wander. Someday all this harassment would be over, and she and Stefan could plan a life together. Of course, he hadn't actually said anything about that, but Elena herself was sure. She was going to marry Stefan, or no one. And Stefan was going to marry no one but her . . .

The transition into dreaming was so smooth and gradual that she scarcely noticed it. But she knew, somehow, that she *was* dreaming. It was as if a little part of her was standing aside and watching the dream like a play.

She was sitting in a long hallway, which was covered with mirrors on one side and windows on the other. She was waiting for something. Then she saw a flicker of movement, and Stefan was standing outside the window. His face was pale and his eyes were hurt and angry. She went over to the window, but she couldn't hear what he was saying because of the glass. In one hand, he was holding a book with a blue velvet cover, and he kept gesturing to it and asking her something. Then he dropped the book and turned away.

"Stefan, don't go! Don't leave me!" she cried. Her fingers flattened whitely on the glass. Then she noticed that there was a latch on one side of the window and she opened it, calling to him. But he had disappeared and outside she saw only swirling white mist.

Disconsolately, she turned away from the window and began walking down the hall. Her own image glimmered in mirror after mirror as she went by them. Then something about one of the reflections caught her eye. The eyes were her eyes, but there was a new look in them, a predatory, sly look. Vickie's eyes had looked that way when she was undressing. And there was something disturbing and hungry about her smile.

As she watched, standing still, the image suddenly whirled around and around, as if dancing. Horror swept over Elena. She began to run down the hall, but now all the reflections had a life of their own, dancing, beckoning to her, laughing at her. Just when she thought her heart and lungs would burst with terror, she reached the end of the corridor and flung open a door.

She was standing in a large and beautiful room. The lofty ceiling was intricately carved and inlaid with gold; the doorways were faced with white marble. Classical statues stood in niches along the walls. Elena had never seen a room of such splendour, but she knew where she was. In Renaissance Italy, when Stefan had been alive.

She looked down at herself and saw she was wearing a dress like the one she'd had made for Hallowe'en, the ice blue Renaissance ball gown. But this dress was a deep ruby red, and around her waist she wore a thin chain set with brilliant red stones. The same stones were in her hair. When she moved, the silk shimmered like flames in the light of hundreds of torches.

At the far end of the room, two huge doors swung inwards. A figure appeared between them. It walked towards her, and she saw that it was a young man dressed in Renaissance clothing, doublet and hose and fur-trimmed jerkin.

Stefan! She started towards him eagerly, feeling the weight of her dress swing from the waist. But when she got closer she stopped, drawing in a sharp breath. It was Damon.

He kept on walking towards her, confident, casual.

He was smiling, a smile of challenge. Reaching her, he put one hand over his heart and bowed. Then he held out the hand to her as if daring her to take it.

"Do you like dancing?" he said. Except that his lips didn't move. The voice was in her mind.

Her fear drained away, and she laughed. What was wrong with her, to have ever been afraid of him? They understood each other very well. But instead of taking his hand, she turned away, the silk of the dress turning after her. She moved lightly towards one of the statues along the wall, not glancing back to see if he was following her. She knew he would. She pretended to be absorbed in the statue, moving away again just as he reached her, biting her lip to hold in the laughter. She felt wonderful right now, so alive, so beautiful. Dangerous? Of course, this game was dangerous. But she had always enjoyed danger.

The next time he drew near her, she glanced at him teasingly as she turned. He reached out, but caught only the jewelled chain at her waist. He let go quickly, and, looking back, she saw that the pronged setting on one of the gems had cut him.

The drop of blood on his finger was just the colour of her dress. His eyes flashed at her sideways, and his lips curved in a taunting smile as he held the wounded finger up. You wouldn't dare, those eyes said.

Oh, wouldn't I? Elena told him with her own eyes. Boldly, she took his hand and held it a moment, teasing him. Then she brought the finger to her lips.

After a few moments, she released it and looked up at him. "I do like dancing," she said, and found that, like him, she could speak with her mind. It was a thrilling sensation. She moved to the centre of the room and waited.

He followed her, graceful as a stalking beast. His fingers were warm and hard when they clasped hers.

There was music, although it faded in and out and sounded far away. Damon placed his other hand on her waist. She could feel the warmth of his fingers there, the pressure. She picked up her skirts, and they began dancing.

It was lovely, like flying, and her body knew every move to make. They danced around and around that empty room, in perfect timing, together.

He was laughing down at her, his dark eyes glittering with enjoyment. She felt so beautiful; so poised and alert and ready for anything. She couldn't remember when she'd had this much fun.

Gradually, though, his smile faded, and their dancing slowed. At last she stood unmoving in the circle of his arms. His dark eyes were not amused any longer, but fierce and heated. She looked up at him soberly, unafraid. And then for the first time she felt as if she *were* dreaming; she felt slightly dizzy and very languid and weak.

The room around her was blurring. She could see only his eyes, and they were making her feel more and more sleepy. She allowed her own eyes to half close, her head to fall back. She sighed.

She could *feel* his gaze now, on her lips, on her throat. She smiled to herself and let her eyes close completely.

He was supporting her weight now, keeping her from falling down. She felt his lips on the skin of her neck, burning hot as if he had a fever. Then she felt the sting, like the jabs of two needles. It was over quickly, though, and she relaxed to the pleasure of having her blood drawn out.

She remembered this feeling, the feeling of floating on a bed of golden light. A delicious languor stole through all her limbs. She felt drowsy, as if it were too much trouble to move. She didn't want to move anyway; she felt too good.

Her fingers were resting on his hair, clasping his head to her. Idly, she threaded them through the soft dark strands. His hair was like silk, warm and alive under her fingers. When she opened her eyes a slit, she saw that it reflected rainbows in the candlelight. Red and blue and purple, just like – just like the feathers . . .

And then everything shattered. There was pain at her throat suddenly, as if her soul was being torn out of her. She was pushing at Damon, clawing at him, trying to force him away. Screams rang in her ears. Damon was fighting her, but it wasn't Damon; it was a crow. Huge wings beat against her, thrashing in the air.

Her eyes were open. She was awake and screaming. The ballroom was gone, and she was in a darkened bedroom. But the nightmare had followed her. Even as she reached for the light, it came at her again, wings thrashing in her face, sharp beak diving for her.

Elena struck out at it, one hand flung up to protect

her eyes. She was still screaming. She couldn't get away from it, those terrible wings kept flailing frantically, with a sound like a thousand decks of cards being shuffled at once.

The door burst open, and she heard shouts. The warm, heavy body of the crow struck her and her screams went higher. Then someone was pulling her off the bed, and she was standing protected behind Bonnie's father. He had a broom and he was beating at the bird with it.

Bonnie was standing in the doorway. Elena ran into her arms. Bonnie's father was shouting, and then came the slam of a window.

"It's out," Mr McCullough said, breathing hard.

Mary and Mrs McCullough were just outside in the hallway, clad in bathrobes. "You're hurt," Mrs McCullough said to Elena in amazement. "The nasty thing's pecked you."

"I'm OK," Elena said, brushing at a spot of blood on her face. She was so shaken that her knees were about to give out.

"How did it get *in*?" said Bonnie.

Mr McCullough was inspecting the window. "You shouldn't have left this open," he said. "And what did you want to take the locks off for?"

"I didn't," Elena cried.

"It was unlocked and open when I heard you screaming and came in," Bonnie's father said. "I don't know who else could have opened it but you."

Elena choked back her protests. Hesitantly, cautiously, she moved to the window. He was right;

the locks had been unscrewed. And it could have been done only from the inside.

"Maybe you were sleepwalking," said Bonnie, leading Elena away from the window as Mr McCullough began putting the locks back on. "We'd better get you cleaned up."

Sleepwalking. Suddenly the entire dream flooded back to Elena. The hall of mirrors, and the ballroom, and Damon. Dancing with Damon. She pulled out of Bonnie's grasp.

"I'll do it myself," she said, hearing her own voice quaver on the edge of hysteria. "No – really – I want to." She escaped into the bathroom and stood with her back to the locked door, trying to breathe.

The last thing she wanted to do was look in a mirror. But at last, slowly, she approached the one over the sink, trembling as she saw the edge of her reflection, moving inch by inch until she was framed in the silvery surface.

Her image stared back, ghastly pale, with eyes that looked bruised and frightened. There were deep shadows under them and smears of blood on her face.

Slowly, she turned her head slightly and lifted up her hair. She almost cried out loud when she saw what was underneath.

Two little wounds, fresh and open on the skin of her neck.

CHAPTER

9

"I know I'm going to be sorry I asked this," Matt said, turning red-rimmed eyes from their contemplation of 1–95 to Stefan in the passenger seat beside him. "But can you tell me *why* we want these extra-special, not-available-locally, semi-tropical weeds for Elena?"

Stefan looked into the back seat at the results of their search through hedgerows and rough grass. The plants, with their branching green stems and their small-toothed leaves, did look more like weeds than anything else. The dried remains of blossoms at the ends of the shoots were almost invisible, and no one could pretend the shoots themselves were decorative.

"What if I said they could be used to make an all-natural eyewash?" he offered, after a moment's thought. "Or a herbal tea?"

"Why? Were you thinking of saying something like that?"

"Not really."

"Good. Because if you did I'd probably deck you."

Without actually looking at Matt, Stefan smiled. There was something new stirring inside him, something he hadn't felt for nearly five centuries, except with Elena. Acceptance. Warmth and friendship shared with a fellow being, who did not know the truth about him, but who trusted him anyway. Who was willing to take him on faith. He wasn't sure he deserved it, but he couldn't deny what it meant to him. It almost made him feel . . . human again.

Elena stared at her image in the mirror. It hadn't been a dream. Not entirely. The wounds in her neck proved that. And now that she'd seen them, she noticed the feeling of light-headedness, of lethargy.

It was her own fault. She'd taken so much trouble to warn Bonnie and Meredith not to invite any strangers into their houses. And all the time she'd forgotten that she herself had invited Damon into Bonnie's house. She'd done it that night she had set up the dumb supper in Bonnie's dining room and called out into the darkness, "Come in."

And the invitation was good for ever. He could return any time he liked, even now. Especially now, while she was weak and might easily be hypnotised into unlocking a window again.

Elena stumbled out of the bathroom, past Bonnie, and into the guest bedroom. She grabbed her tote bag and began stuffing things into it.

"Elena, you can't go home!"

"I can't stay here," Elena said. She looked around for her shoes, spotted them by the bed, and started forwards. Then she stopped, with a strangled sound. Lying on the dainty crumpled linen of the bed there was a single black feather. It was huge, horribly huge and real and solid, with a thick, waxy-looking shaft. It looked almost obscene resting there on the white sheets.

Nausea swept over Elena, and she turned away. She couldn't breathe.

"OK, OK," Bonnie said. "If you feel that way about it, I'll get Dad to take you home."

"You have to come, too." It had just dawned on Elena that Bonnie was no safer in this house than she was. *You and your loved ones*, she remembered, and turned to grasp Bonnie's arm. "You *have* to, Bonnie. I need you with me."

And at last she got her way. The McCulloughs thought she was hysterical, that she was overreacting, possibly that she was having a nervous breakdown. But finally they gave in. Mr McCullough drove her and Bonnie to the Gilbert house, where, feeling like burglars, they unlocked the door and crept inside without waking anyone up.

Even here, Elena couldn't sleep. She lay beside Bonnie's softly breathing form, staring towards her bedroom window, watching. Outside, the quince branches squeaked against the glass, but nothing else moved until dawn.

That was when she heard the car. She'd know the wheezing sound of Matt's engine anywhere. Alarmed, she tiptoed to the window and looked out into the early-morning stillness of another grey day. Then she hurried downstairs and opened the front door.

"Stefan!" She had never been so glad to see anyone in her life. She flung herself upon him before he could even shut the car door. He swayed backwards with the force of her impact, and she could feel his surprise. She wasn't usually so demonstrative in public.

"Hey," he said, returning the hug gently. "Me, too, but don't crush the flowers."

"Flowers?" She pulled back to look at what he was carrying; then, she looked at his face. Then at Matt, who was emerging from the other side of the car. Stefan's face was pale and drawn; Matt's was puffy with tiredness, with bloodshot eyes.

"You'd better come inside," she said at last, bewildered. "You both look awful."

"It's vervain," said Stefan, some time later. He and Elena were sitting at the kitchen table. Through the open doorway, Matt could be seen stretched out on the family room sofa, snoring gently. He'd flopped there after eating three bowls of cereal. Aunt Judith, Bonnie and Margaret were still upstairs asleep, but Stefan kept his voice low just the same. "You remember what I told you about it?" he said.

"You said it helps keep your mind clear even when someone is using Power to influence it." Elena was proud of how steady her voice was.

"Right. And that's one of the things Damon might

try. He can use the power of his mind even from a distance, and he can do it whether you're awake or asleep."

Tears filled Elena's eyes, and she looked down to hide them, gazing at the long slender stems with the dried remains of tiny lilac flowers at the very tips. "Asleep?" she said, afraid that this time her voice was not as steady.

"Yes. He could influence you to come out of the house, say, or to let him in. But the vervain should prevent that." Stefan sounded tired, but satisfied with himself.

Oh, Stefan, if you only knew, Elena thought. The gift had come one night too late. In spite of all her efforts, a tear fell, dripping on to the long green leaves.

"Elena!" He sounded startled. "What is it? Tell me."

He was trying to look into her face, but she bowed her head, pressing it into his shoulder. He put his arms around her, not trying to force her up again. "Tell me," he repeated softly.

This was the moment. If she was ever going to tell him, it should be now. Her throat felt burned and swollen, and she wanted to let all the words inside pour out.

But she couldn't. No matter what, I won't let them fight over me, she thought.

"It's just that – I was worried about you," she managed. "I didn't know where you'd gone, or when you were coming back."

"I should have told you. But that's all? There's nothing else upsetting you?"

"That's all." Now she would have to swear Bonnie to secrecy about the crow. Why did one lie always lead to another? "What should we do with the vervain?" she asked, sitting back.

"I'll show you tonight. Once I've extracted the oil from the seeds, you can rub it into your skin or add it to a bath. And you can make the dried leaves into a sachet and carry it with you or put it under your pillow at night."

"I'd better give them to Bonnie and Meredith, too. They'll need protection."

He nodded. "For now—" He broke off a sprig and placed it in her hand. "—just take this to school with you. I'm going back to the boarding house to extract the oil." He paused for a moment and then spoke. "Elena . . ."

"Yes?"

"If I thought it would do you any good, I'd leave. I wouldn't expose you to Damon. But I don't think he'd follow me if I went, not any more. I think he might stay – because of you."

"Don't even *think* about leaving," she said fiercely, looking up at him. "Stefan, that's the one thing I couldn't stand. Promise you won't; promise me."

"I won't leave you alone with him," Stefan said, which was not quite the same thing. But there was no point in pushing him further.

Instead, she helped him wake up Matt, and saw them both off. Then, with a stem of dried vervain in her hand, she went upstairs to get ready for school.

Bonnie yawned all the way through breakfast, and

she didn't really wake up until they were outside, walking to school with a brisk breeze in their faces. It was going to be a cold day.

"I had a very weird dream last night," Bonnie said.

Elena's heart jumped. She'd already tucked a sprig of vervain into Bonnie's backpack, down at the bottom, where Bonnie wouldn't see it. But if Damon had got to Bonnie last night . . .

"What about?" she said, bracing herself.

"About you. I saw you standing under a tree and the wind was blowing. For some reason, I was afraid of you, and I didn't want to go any closer. You looked . . . different. Very pale but almost glowing. And then a crow flew down from the tree, and you reached out and grabbed it in midair. You were so fast it was unbelievable. And then you looked over at me, with this expression. You were smiling, but it made me want to run. And then you twisted the crow's neck, and it was dead."

Elena had listened to this with growing horror. Now she said, "That's a *disgusting* dream."

"It is, isn't it?" said Bonnie composedly. "I wonder what it means? Crows are birds of ill omen in the legends. They can foretell a death."

"It probably meant that you knew how upset I was, finding that crow in the room."

"Yes," Bonnie said. "Except for one thing. I had this dream *before* you woke us all up screaming."

That day at lunchtime there was another piece of violet paper on the office notice board. This one, though, read simply: *LOOK IN PERSONALS*.

"What personals?" said Bonnie.

Meredith, walking up at that moment with a copy of the *Wildcat Weekly*, the school newspaper, provided the answer. "Have you seen this?" she said.

It was in the personals section, completely anonymous, with neither salutation nor signature. *I can't bear the thought of losing him. But he's so very unhappy about something, and if he won't tell me what it is, if he won't trust me that much, I don't see any hope for us.*

Reading it, Elena felt a burst of new energy through her tiredness. Oh, God, she hated whoever was doing this. She imagined shooting them, stabbing them, watching them fall. And then, vividly, she imagined something else. Yanking back a fistful of the thief's hair and sinking her teeth into an unprotected throat. It was a strange, unsettling vision, but for a moment it almost seemed real.

She became aware that Bonnie and Meredith were looking at her.

"Well?" she said, feeling slightly uncomfortable.

"I could tell you weren't listening," sighed Bonnie. "I just said it still doesn't look like Da— like the killer's work to me. It doesn't seem like a murderer would be so petty."

"Much as I hate to agree with her, she's right," Meredith said. "This smells like someone sneaky. Someone who has a grudge against you personally and who really wants to make you suffer."

Saliva had collected in Elena's mouth, and she swallowed. "Also somebody who's familiar with the school. They had to fill out a form for a personals message in one of the journalism classes," she said.

"And somebody who knew you kept a diary, assuming they stole it on purpose. Maybe they were in one of your classes that day you took it to school. Remember? When Mr Tanner almost caught you," Bonnie added.

"Ms Halpern *did* catch me; she even read some of it aloud, a bit about Stefan. That was right after Stefan and I got together. Wait a minute, Bonnie. That night at your house when the diary was stolen, how long were you two out of the living room?"

"Just a few minutes. Yangtze had stopped barking, and I went to the door to let him in, and . . ." Bonnie pressed her lips together and shrugged.

"So the thief had to be familiar with your house," said Meredith swiftly, "or he or she wouldn't have been able to get in, get the diary, and get out again before we saw them. All right, then, we're looking for someone sneaky and cruel, probably in one of your classes, Elena, and most likely familiar with Bonnie's house. Someone who has a personal grudge and will stoop to anything to get you . . . Oh, my God."

The three of them stared at one another.

"It has to be," whispered Bonnie. "It has to."

"We're so stupid; we should have seen it right away," said Meredith.

For Elena, it meant the sudden realisation that all the anger she'd felt about this before was nothing to the anger she was capable of feeling. A candle flame to the sun.

"Caroline," she said, and clenched her teeth so hard her jaw hurt.

Caroline. Elena actually felt she could kill the green-eyed girl right now. And she might have rushed out to try if Bonnie and Meredith hadn't stopped her.

"After school," said Meredith firmly, "when we can take her somewhere private. Just wait that long, Elena."

But as they headed for the cafeteria, Elena noticed an auburn head disappearing down the art and music corridor. And she remembered something Stefan had said earlier this year, about Caroline taking him into the photography room at lunchtime. For privacy, Caroline had told him.

"You two go on; I forgot something," she said as soon as Bonnie and Meredith both had food on their cafeteria trays. Then she pretended to be deaf as she walked rapidly out and backtracked to the art wing.

All the rooms were dark, but the photography room's door was unlocked. Something made Elena turn the knob cautiously, and move quietly once she was inside, rather than marching in to start a confrontation as she'd planned. Was Caroline in here? If so, what was she doing alone in the dark?

The room appeared at first to be deserted. Then Elena heard the murmur of voices from a small alcove at the back, and she saw that the darkroom door was ajar.

Silently, stealthily, she made her way until she stood just outside the doorway, and the murmur of sound resolved itself into words.

"But how can we be sure she'll be the one they pick?" That was Caroline.

"My father's on the school board. They'll pick her, all right." And *that* was Tyler Smallwood. His father was a lawyer, and on every board there was. "Besides, who else would it be?" he continued. " 'The Spirit of Fell's Church' is supposed to be brainy as well as build."

"And *I* don't have brains, I suppose?"

"Did I say that? Look, if you want to be the one to parade in a white dress on Founders' Day, fine. But if you want to see Stefan Salvatore run out of town on the evidence of his own girlfriend's diary . . ."

"But why wait so long?"

Tyler sounded impatient. "Because this way it'll ruin the celebration, too. The *Fells'* celebration. Why should *they* get the credit for founding this town? The Smallwoods were here first."

"Oh, who cares about who founded the town? All I want is to see Elena humiliated in front of the entire school."

"And Salvatore." The pure hatred and malice in Tyler's voice made Elena's flesh crawl. "He'll be lucky if he doesn't end up hanging from a tree. You're sure the evidence is there?"

"How many times do I have to tell you? First, it says she lost the ribbon on the second of September in the cemetery. Then, it says Stefan picked it up that day and kept it. Wickery Bridge is right beside the cemetery. That means Stefan was near the bridge on the second of September, the night the old man was attacked there. Everybody already knows he was on hand for the attacks on Vickie and Tanner. What more do you want?"

"It would never stand up in court. Maybe I should get some corroborating evidence. Like ask old Mrs Flowers what time he got home that night."

"Oh, who *cares*? Most people think he's guilty already. The diary talks about some big secret he's hiding from everyone. People will get the idea."

"You're keeping it in a safe place?"

"No, Tyler, I'm keeping it out on the coffee table. How stupid do you think I am?"

"Stupid enough to send Elena notes tipping her off." There was a crackle, as of newspaper. "Look at this, this is unbelievable. And it's got to stop, *now*. What if she figures out who's doing it?"

"What's she going to do about it, call the police?"

"I still want you to lay off. Just wait until Founders' Day; then you'll get to watch the Ice Princess melt."

"And to say *ciao* to Stefan. Tyler . . . nobody's really going to hurt him, are they?"

"Who *cares*?" Tyler mocked her earlier tone. "You leave that to me and my friends, Caroline. You just do your part, OK?"

Caroline's voice dropped to a throaty murmur. "Convince me." After a pause Tyler chuckled.

There was movement, rustling sounds, a sigh. Elena turned and slipped out of the room as quietly as she had come in.

She got into the next hallway, and then she leaned against the lockers there, trying to think.

It was almost too much to absorb at once. Caroline,

who had once been her best friend, had betrayed her and wanted to see her humiliated in front of the whole school. Tyler, who'd always seemed more an annoying jerk than a real threat, was planning to get Stefan driven out of town – or killed. And the worst thing was that they were using Elena's own diary to do it.

Now she understood the beginning of her dream last night. She'd had a dream like it the day before she had discovered that Stefan was missing. In both, Stefan had looked at her with angry, accusing eyes, and then he had thrown a book at her feet and walked away.

Not a book. Her diary. Which had in it evidence that could be deadly to Stefan. Three times people in Fell's Church had been attacked, and three times Stefan had been on the scene. What would that look like to the town, to the police?

And there was no way to tell the truth. Supposing she said, "Stefan isn't guilty. It's his brother Damon who hates him and who knows how much Stefan hates even the thought of hurting and killing. And who followed Stefan around and attacked people to make Stefan think maybe Stefan had done it, to drive him mad. And who's here in town *somewhere* – look for him in the cemetery or in the woods. But, oh, by the way, don't just search for a good-looking guy, because he might be a crow at the moment.

"Incidentally, he's a vampire."

She didn't even believe it herself. It sounded ludicrous.

A twinge from the side of her neck reminded her

how serious the ludicrous story really was. She felt odd today, almost as if she were sick. It was more than just tension and lack of sleep. She felt slightly dizzy, and at times the ground seemed to be spongy, giving way under her feet and then springing back. Flu symptoms, except that she was sure they weren't due to any *virus* in her bloodstream.

Damon's fault, again. Everything was Damon's fault, except the diary. She had no one to blame for that but herself. If only she hadn't written about Stefan, if only she hadn't brought the diary to school. If only she hadn't left it in Bonnie's living room. If only, if only.

Right now all that mattered was that she had to get it back.

The bell rang. There was no time to go back to the cafeteria and tell Bonnie and Meredith. Elena set off for her next class, past the averted faces and hostile eyes that were becoming all too familiar these days.

It was hard, in history class, not to stare at Caroline, not to let Caroline know she knew. Alaric asked about Matt and Stefan being absent for the second day in a row, and Elena shrugged, feeling exposed and on display. She didn't trust this man with the boyish smile and the hazel eyes and the thirst for knowledge about Mr Tanner's death. And Bonnie, who simply gazed at Alaric soulfully, was no help at all.

After class she caught a scrap of Sue Carson's conversation. "... he's on vacation from college – I forget exactly where ..."

Elena had had enough of discreet silence. She spun

VAMPIRE DIARIES

around and spoke directly to Sue and the girl Sue was talking to, bursting uninvited into their discussion.

"If I were you," she said to Sue, "I would keep away from Damon. I mean that."

There was startled, embarrassed laughter. Sue was one of the few people at school who hadn't shunned Elena, and now she was looking as if she wished she had.

"You mean," said the other girl hesitantly, "because he's yours, too? Or—"

Elena's own laughter was harsh. "I mean because he's *dangerous*," she said. "And I'm not joking."

They just looked at her. Elena saved them the further embarrassment of having to reply or to get tactfully away by turning on her heel and leaving. She collected Bonnie from Alaric's cluster of after-school groupies and headed for Meredith's locker.

"Where are we going? I thought we were going to talk to Caroline."

"Not any more," Elena said. "Wait until we get home. Then I'll tell you why."

"I can't believe it," said Bonnie an hour later. "I mean, I believe it, but I can't *believe* it. Not even of Caroline."

"It's Tyler," Elena said. "He's the one with the big plans. So much for men not being interested in diaries."

"Actually, we should thank him," said Meredith. "Because of him at least we have until Founders' Day to do something about it. *Why* did you say it was supposed to be on Founders' Day, Elena?"

"Tyler has something against the Fells."

"But they're all dead," said Bonnie.

"Well, that doesn't seem to matter to Tyler. I remember him talking about it in the graveyard, too, when we were looking at their tomb. He thinks they stole his ancestors' rightful place as the town's founders or something."

"Elena," Meredith said seriously, "is there anything else in the diary that could hurt Stefan? Besides the thing about the old man, I mean."

"Isn't that enough?" With those steady, dark eyes on her, Elena felt discomfort flutter between her ribs. What was Meredith asking?

"Enough to get Stefan run out of town like they said," agreed Bonnie.

"Enough that we have to get the diary back from Caroline," Elena said. "The only question is, how?"

"Caroline said she had it hidden somewhere safe. That probably means her house." Meredith chewed her lip thoughtfully. "She's got just the one brother in eighth grade, right? And her mum doesn't work, but she goes shopping in Roanoke a lot. Do they still have a maid?"

"Why?" said Bonnie. "What difference does it make?"

"Well, we don't want anybody walking in while we're burgling the house."

"While we're *what*?" Bonnie's voice rose to a squeak. "You can't be serious!"

"What are we supposed to do, just sit back and wait until Founders' Day, and let her read Elena's diary in front of the town? *She* stole it from *your* house. We've just got to steal it back," Meredith said, maddeningly calm.

"We'll get caught. We'll get expelled from school – if we don't end up going to jail." Bonnie turned to Elena in appeal. "Tell her, Elena."

"Well . . ." In all honesty, the prospect made Elena herself a little queasy. It wasn't so much the idea of expulsion, or even jail, as just the thought of being caught in the act. Mrs Forbes's haughty face floated before her eyes, full of righteous indignation. Then it changed to Caroline's, laughing spitefully as her mother pointed an accusing finger right at Elena.

Besides, it seemed such a . . . a *violation*, to go into someone's house when they were not there, to search their possessions. She would hate it if someone did that to her.

But, of course, someone had. Caroline had violated Bonnie's house, and right now had Elena's most private possession in her hands.

"Let's do it," Elena said quietly. "But let's be careful."

"Can't we talk about this?" said Bonnie weakly, looking from Meredith's determined face to Elena's.

"There's nothing to talk about. You're coming," Meredith told her. "You promised," she added, as Bonnie took a breath to object afresh. And she held up her index finger.

"The blood oath was only to help Elena *get* Stefan!" Bonnie cried.

"Think again," said Meredith. "You swore you

would do whatever Elena asked in relation to Stefan. There wasn't anything about a time limit or about 'only until Elena gets him'."

Bonnie's mouth dropped open. She looked at Elena, who was almost laughing in spite of herself. "It's true," Elena said solemnly. "And you said it yourself: 'Swearing with blood means you have to stick to your oath no matter what happens.' "

Bonnie shut her mouth and thrust her chin out. "Right," she said grimly. "Now I'm stuck for the rest of my life doing whatever Elena wants me to do about Stefan. Wonderful."

"This is the last thing I'll ever ask," Elena said. "And *I* promise that. I swear—"

"Don't!" said Meredith, suddenly serious. "Don't, Elena. You might be sorry later."

"Now you're taking up prophecy, too?" Elena said. And then she asked, "So how are we going to get hold of Caroline's house key for an hour or so?"

9 November, Saturday
Dear Diary,

I'm sorry it's been so long. Lately I've been too busy or too depressed – or both – to write you.

Besides, with everything that's happened I'm almost afraid to keep a diary at all any more. But I need someone to turn to, because right now there's not a single human being, not a single person on earth, that I'm not keeping something from.

Bonnie and Meredith can't know the truth about Stefan. Stefan can't know the truth about Damon. Aunt Judith can't know about anything. Bonnie and Meredith know about Caroline and the diary; Stefan doesn't. Stefan knows about the vervain I use every day now; Bonnie and Meredith don't. Even though I've given both of them sachets full of the stuff. One good thing: it seems to work, or at least I haven't been sleepwalking again since that night. But it would be a lie to say I haven't been dreaming about Damon. He's in all my nightmares.

My life is full of lies right now, and I need someone to be completely honest with. I'm going to hide this diary under the loose floorboard in the closet, so that no one will find it even if I drop dead and they clean out my room. Maybe one of Margaret's grandchildren will be playing in there someday, and will pry up the board and pull it out, but until then, nobody. This diary is my last secret.

I don't know why I'm thinking about death and dying. That's Bonnie's craze; she's the one who thinks it would be so romantic. I know what it's really like; there was nothing romantic about it when Mum and Dad died. Just the worst feeling in the world. I want to live for a good long time, marry Stefan, and be happy. And there's no reason why I can't, once all of these problems are behind us.

Except that there are times when I get scared and I don't believe that. And there are little things that shouldn't matter, but they bother me. Like why Stefan still wears Katherine's ring around his neck, even though I know he loves me. Like why he's never said he loves me, even though I know it's true.

It doesn't matter. Everything will work out. It has to work out. And then we'll be together and be happy. There's no reason why we can't. There's no reason why we can't. There's no reason

Elena stopped writing, trying to keep the letters on the page in focus. But they only blurred further, and she shut the book before a betraying teardrop could fall on the ink. Then she went over to the closet, pried up the loose board with a nail file, and put the diary there.

She had the nail file in her pocket a week later as the three of them, she and Bonnie and Meredith, stood outside Caroline's back door.

"Hurry up," hissed Bonnie in agony, looking around the yard as if she expected something to jump out at them. "Come on, Meredith!"

"There," said Meredith, as the key finally went the right way into the lock and the doorknob yielded to her turning fingers. "We're in."

"Are you sure *they're* not in? Elena, what if they come back early? Why couldn't we do this in the daytime, at least?"

"Bonnie, will you get *inside*? We've been through all of this. The maid's always here in the daytime. And they won't be back early tonight unless somebody gets sick at Chez Louis. Now, come on!" said Elena.

"Nobody would dare to get sick at Mr Forbes's birthday dinner," Meredith said comfortingly to Bonnie as the smaller girl stepped in. "We're safe."

"If they've got enough money to go to expensive restaurants, you'd think they could afford to leave a few lights on," said Bonnie, refusing to be comforted.

Privately, Elena agreed with this. It was strange and disconcerting to be wandering through someone else's house in the dark, and her heart pounded chokingly as they went up the stairs. Her palm, clutching the key chain torch that showed the way, was wet and slippery. But in spite of these physical symptoms of panic, her mind was still operating coolly, almost with detachment.

"It's got to be in her bedroom," she said.

Caroline's window faced the street, which meant they had to be even more careful not to show a light there. Elena swung the tiny beam of the torch around with a feeling of dismay. It was one thing to plan to search someone's room, to picture efficiently and methodically going through drawers. It was another thing to be actually standing here, surrounded by what seemed like thousands of places to hide something, and feeling afraid to touch anything in case Caroline noticed that it had been disturbed.

The other two girls were also standing still.

"Maybe we should just go home," Bonnie said quietly. And Meredith did not contradict her.

"We have to try. At least try," said Elena, hearing how tinny and hollow her voice sounded. She eased open a drawer in the chest of drawers and shone the light on to dainty piles of lacy underwear. A moment's poking through them assured her there was nothing like a book there. She straightened the piles and shut the drawer again. Then she let out her breath.

"It's not that hard," she said. "What we need to do

is divide up the room and then search *everything* in our section, every drawer, every piece of furniture, every object big enough to hide a diary in."

She assigned herself the closet, and the first thing she did was prod at the floorboards with her nail file. But Caroline's boards all seemed to be secure and the walls of the wardrobe sounded solid. Rummaging through Caroline's clothes she found several things she'd lent the other girl last year. She was tempted to take them back, but of course she couldn't. A search of Caroline's shoes and purses revealed nothing, even when she dragged a chair over so that she could investigate the top shelf of the wardrobe thoroughly.

Meredith was sitting on the floor examining a pile of stuffed animals that had been relegated to a chest with other childish mementos. She ran her long sensitive fingers over each, checking for slits in the material. When she reached a fluffy poodle, she paused.

"I gave this to her," she whispered. "I think for her tenth birthday. I thought she'd thrown it away."

Elena couldn't see her eyes; Meredith's own torch was turned on the poodle. But she knew how Meredith was feeling.

"I tried to make up with her," she said softly. "I did, Meredith, at the Haunted House. But she as good as told me she would never forgive me for taking Stefan from her. I wish things could be different, but she won't let them be."

"So now it's war."

"So now it's war," said Elena, flat and final. She

watched as Meredith put the poodle aside and picked up the next animal. Then she turned back to her own search.

But she had no better luck with the dresser than she had with the closet. And with every moment that passed she felt more uneasy, more certain that they were about to hear a car pulling into the Forbes' driveway.

"It's no use," Meredith said at last, feeling underneath Caroline's mattress. "She must have hidden it . . . wait. There's something here. I can feel a corner."

Elena and Bonnie stared from opposite ends of the room, momentarily frozen.

"I've got it. Elena, it's a diary!"

Relief swooped through Elena then, and she felt like a crumpled piece of paper being straightened and smoothed. She could move again. Breathing was wonderful. She'd known, she'd known all along that nothing *really* terrible could happen to Stefan. Life couldn't be that cruel, not to Elena Gilbert. They were all safe now.

But Meredith's voice was puzzled. "It's a diary. But it's green, not blue. It's the wrong one."

"*What?*" Elena snatched the little book, shining her light on it, trying to make the emerald green of the cover change into sapphire blue. It didn't work. This diary was almost exactly like hers, but it wasn't hers.

"It's Caroline's," she said stupidly, still not wanting to believe it.

Bonnie and Meredith crowded close. They all

looked at the closed book, and then at one another.

"There might be clues," said Elena slowly.

"It's only fair," agreed Meredith. But it was Bonnie who actually took the diary and opened it.

Elena peered over her shoulder at Caroline's spiky back-slanted writing, so different from the block letters of the purple notes. At first her eyes wouldn't focus, but then a name leapt out at her. *Elena*.

"Wait, what's that?"

Bonnie, who was the only one actually in a position to read more than one or two words, was silent a moment, her lips moving. Then she snorted.

"Listen to this," she said, and read: " 'Elena's the most selfish person I've ever known. Everyone thinks she's so together, but it's really just coldness. It's sickening the way people suck up to her, never realising that she doesn't give a damn about anyone or anything except Elena.' "

"*Caroline* says that? She should talk!" But Elena could feel heat in her face. It was, practically, what Matt had said about her when she was after Stefan.

"Go on, there's more," said Meredith, poking at Bonnie, who continued in an offended voice.

" 'Bonnie's almost as bad these days, always trying to make herself important. The newest thing is pretending she's psychic so people will pay attention to her. If she was *really* psychic she'd figure out that Elena is just using her.' "

There was a heavy pause, and then Elena said, "Is that all?"

"No, there's a bit about Meredith. 'Meredith

doesn't do anything to stop it. In fact, Meredith doesn't *do* anything; she just watches. It's as if she can't act; she can only *react* to things. Besides, I've heard my parents talking about her family – no wonder she never mentions them.' What's that supposed to mean?"

Meredith hadn't moved, and Elena could see only her neck and chin in the dim light. But she spoke quietly and steadily. "It doesn't matter. Keep on looking, Bonnie, for something about Elena's diary."

"Try around the eighteenth of October. That was when it was stolen," said Elena, putting her questions aside. She'd ask Meredith about it later.

There was no entry for the eighteenth of October or the weekend after; in fact, there were only a few entries for the following weeks. None of them mentioned the diary.

"Well, that's it then," said Meredith, sitting back. "This book is useless. Unless we want to blackmail *her* with it. You know, like we won't show hers if she won't show yours."

It was a tempting idea, but Bonnie spotted the flaw. "There's nothing bad about Caroline in here; it's all just complaints about other people. Mostly us. I'll bet Caroline would *love* to have it read out loud in front of the whole school. It'd make her day."

"So what do we do with it?"

"Put it back," said Elena tiredly. She swung her light around the room, which seemed to her eyes to be filled with subtle differences from when they'd come in. "We'll just have to keep on pretending we don't know she has my diary, and hope for another chance."

"All right," said Bonnie, but she went on thumbing through the little book, occasionally giving vent to an indignant snort or hiss. "Will you listen to this!" she exclaimed.

"There isn't time," Elena said. She would have said something else, but at that moment Meredith spoke, her tone commanding everyone's immediate attention.

"A car."

It took only a second to ascertain that the vehicle was pulling up into the Forbes' driveway. Bonnie's eyes and mouth were wide and round and she seemed to be paralysed, kneeling by the bed.

"Go! Go on," said Elena, snatching the diary from her. "Turn the torches off and get out the back door."

They were already moving, Meredith urging Bonnie forwards. Elena dropped to her knees and lifted the bedspread, pulling up at Caroline's mattress. With her other hand she pushed the diary, wedging it between the mattress and the valence. The thinly covered box springs bit into her arm from below, but even worse was the weight of the queen-size mattress bearing down from above. She gave the book a few more nudges with her fingertips and then pulled her arm out, tugging the bedspread back in place.

She gave one wild glance back at the room as she left; there was no time to fix anything more now. As she moved swiftly and silently toward the stairs, she heard a key in the front door.

What followed was a sort of dreadful game of tag. Elena knew they were not deliberately chasing her, but the Forbes family seemed determined to corner her in their house. She turned back the way she had come as voices and lights materialised in the hall as they headed up the stairs. She fled from them into the last doorway down the hall, and they seemed to follow. They moved across the landing; they were right outside the master bedroom. She turned towards the adjoining bathroom, but then saw lights spring to life under the closed door, cutting off her escape.

She was trapped. At any moment Caroline's parents might come in. She saw the French windows leading to a balcony and made her decision in that same instant.

Outside, the air was cool, and her panting breath showed faintly. Yellow light burst forth from the room beside her, and she huddled even farther to the left, keeping out of its path. Then, the sound she had been dreading came with terrible clarity: the snick of a door handle, followed by a billowing of curtains inwards as the French windows opened.

She looked around frantically. It was too far to jump to the ground, and there was nothing to grab hold of to climb down. That left only the roof, but there was nothing to climb up, either. Still, some instinct made her try, and she was on the balcony railing and groping for a handhold above even as a shadow appeared on the filmy curtains. A hand parted them, a figure began to emerge, and then Elena felt something clasping her own hand, locking on her wrist and hauling her upwards. Automatically, she boosted with her feet and felt herself scrambling on to the shingled roof. Trying to calm her ragged breath, she looked over gratefully to see who her rescuer was – and froze.

CHAPTER

11

"The name *is* Salvatore. As in saviour," he said. There was a brief flash of white teeth in the darkness.

Elena looked down. The overhang of the roof obscured the balcony, but she could hear shuffling sounds down there. But they were not the sounds of pursuit, and there was no sign that her companion's words had been overheard. A minute later, she heard the French windows close.

"I thought it was Smith," she said, still looking down into the darkness.

Damon laughed. It was a terribly engaging laugh, without the bitter edge of Stefan's. It made her think of the rainbow lights on the crow's feathers.

Nevertheless, she was not fooled. Charming as he seemed, Damon was dangerous almost beyond imagination. That graceful, lounging body was ten times stronger than a human's. Those lazy dark eyes were adapted to seeing perfectly at night. The long-fingered hand that had pulled her up to the roof could move with impossible quickness. And, most disturbing of all, his mind was the mind of a killer. A predator.

She could feel it just beneath his surface. He was *different* from a human. He had lived so long by hunting and killing that he'd forgotten any other way. And he enjoyed it, not fighting his nature as Stefan did, but glorying in it. He had no morals and no conscience, and she was trapped here with him in the middle of the night.

She settled back on one heel, ready to jump into action at any minute. She ought to be angry with him now, after what he'd done to her in the dream. She was, but there was no point in expressing it. He knew how furious she must be, and he would only laugh at her if she told him.

She watched him quietly, intently, waiting for his next move.

But he didn't move. Those hands that could dart as quickly as striking snakes rested motionlessly on his knees. His expression reminded her of the way he'd looked at her once before. The first time they'd met she'd seen the same guarded, reluctant respect in his eyes – except that then there had also been surprise in them. Now there was none.

"You're not going to scream at me? Or faint?" he said, as if offering her the standard options.

Elena was still watching him. He was much stronger than she was, and faster, but if she needed to she thought she could get to the edge of the roof before he reached her. It was a ten-metre drop if she missed the balcony, but she might decide to risk it. It all depended on Damon.

"I don't faint," she said shortly. "And why should I scream at you? We were playing a game. I was stupid that night and so I lost. You warned me in the graveyard about the consequences."

His lips parted in a quick breath and he looked away. "I may just have to make you my Queen of Shadows," he said, and, speaking almost to himself, he continued: "I've had many companions, girls as young as you and women who were the beauties of Europe. But *you're* the one I want at my side. Ruling, taking what we want when we want it. Feared and worshipped by all the weaker souls. Would that be so bad?"

"I *am* one of the weaker souls," Elena said. "And you and I are enemies, Damon. We can never be anything else."

"Are you sure?" He looked at her, and she could feel the power of his mind as it touched hers, like the brush of those long fingers. But there was no dizziness, no feeling of weakness or succumbing. That afternoon she'd had a long soak, as she always did these days, in a hot bath sprinkled with dried vervain.

Damon's eyes flashed with understanding, but he took the setback with good grace. "What are you doing here?" he said casually.

It was strange, but she felt no need to lie to him. "Caroline took something that belonged to me. A diary. I came to get it back."

A new look flickered in the dark eyes. "Undoubtedly to protect my worthless brother somehow," he said, annoyed.

"Stefan isn't involved in this!"

"Oh, isn't he?" She was afraid he understood more than she meant him to. "Strange, he always seems to be involved when there's trouble. He *creates* problems. Now, if he were out of the picture . . ."

Elena spoke steadily. "If you hurt Stefan again I'll make you sorry. I'll find some way to make you wish you hadn't, Damon. I mean it."

"I see. Well, then, I'll just have to work on *you*, won't I?"

Elena said nothing. She'd talked herself into a corner, agreeing to play this deadly game of his again. She looked away.

"I'm going to have you in the end, you know," he said softly. It was the voice he'd used at the party, when he'd said, "Easy, easy." There was no mockery or malice now; he was simply stating a fact. "By hook or by crook, as you people say – that's a nice phrase – you'll be mine before the next snow flies."

Elena tried to conceal the chill she felt, but she knew he saw anyway.

"Good," he said. "You do have some sense. You're right to be afraid of me; I'm the most dangerous thing you're ever likely to encounter in your life. But just now I have a business proposition for you."

"A *business* proposition?"

"Exactly. You came here to get a diary. But you

haven't got it." He indicated her empty hands. "You failed, didn't you?" When Elena made no reply he went on. "And since you don't want my brother *involved*, he can't help you. But I can. And I will."

"You will?"

"Of course. For a price."

Elena stared at him. Blood flamed in her face. When she managed to get words out, they would come only in a whisper.

"What – *price*?"

A smile gleamed out of the darkness. "A few minutes of your time, Elena. A few drops of your blood. An hour or so spent with me, alone."

"You . . ." Elena couldn't find the right word. Every epithet she knew was too mild.

"I'll have it anyway, eventually," he said in a reasonable tone. "If you're honest, you'll admit that to yourself. Last time wasn't the last. Why not accept that?" His voice dropped to a warm, intimate timbre. "Remember . . ."

"I'd rather cut my throat," she said.

"An intriguing thought. But I can do it so much more enjoyably."

He was laughing at her. Somehow, on top of everything else today, this was too much. "You're disgusting; you know that," she said. "You're sickening." She was shaking now, and she couldn't breathe. "I'd die before I'd give in to you. I'd rather—"

She wasn't sure what made her do it. When she was with Damon a sort of instinct took over her. And at that moment, she did feel that she'd rather risk anything than let him win this time. She noticed, with half her mind, that he was sitting back, relaxed, enjoying the turn his game was taking. The other half of her mind was calculating how far the roof overhung the balcony.

"I'd rather do this," she said, and flung herself sideways.

She was right; he was off guard and couldn't move fast enough to stop her. She felt free space below her feet and spinning terror as she realised the balcony was further back than she'd thought. She was going to miss it.

But she hadn't reckoned on Damon. His hand shot out, not quick enough to keep her on the roof, but keeping her from falling any further. It was as if her weight was nothing to him. Reflexively, Elena grasped the shingled edge of the roof and tried to get a knee up.

His voice was furious. "You little *fool*! If you're that eager to meet death I can introduce you myself."

"Let go of me," said Elena through her teeth. Someone was going to come out on that balcony at any second, she was sure of it. "*Let go of me.*"

"Here and now?" Looking into those unfathomable black eyes, she realised he was serious. If she said yes he would drop her.

"It would be a fast way to end things, wouldn't it?" she said. Her heart was pounding in fear, but she refused to let him see that.

"But such a waste." With one motion, he jerked her to safety. To himself. His arms tightened around her, pressing her to the lean hardness of his body, and suddenly Elena could see nothing. She was enveloped. Then she felt those flat muscles gathering themselves like some great cat's, and the two of them launched into space.

She was falling. She couldn't help but cling to him as the only solid thing in the rushing world around her. Then he landed, catlike, taking the impact easily.

Stefan had done something similar once. But Stefan had not held her this way afterwards, bruisingly close, with his lips almost in contact with hers.

"Think about my proposition," he said.

She could not move or look away. And this time she knew that it was no Power that he was using, but simply the wildfire attraction between them. It was useless to deny it; her body responded to his. She could feel his breath on her lips.

"I don't need you for anything," she told him.

She thought he was going to kiss her then, but he didn't. Above them there was the sound of French windows opening and an angry voice on the balcony. "Hey! What's going on? Is somebody out there?"

"This time I did you a favour," Damon said, very softly, still holding her. "Next time I'm going to collect."

She couldn't have turned her head away. If he'd kissed her then, she would have let him. But suddenly the hardness of his arms melted around her and his face seemed to blur. It was as if the darkness was taking him back into itself. Then black wings caught and beat the air and a huge crow was soaring away.

Something, a book or shoe, was hurled after it from the balcony. It missed by a metre.

"Damn birds!" said Mr Forbes's voice from above. "They must be nesting on the roof."

Shivering, with her arms locked around her, Elena huddled in the darkness below until he went back inside.

She found Meredith and Bonnie crouching by the gate. "What took you so long?" Bonnie whispered. "We thought you were caught!"

"I almost was. I had to stay until it was safe." Elena was so used to lying about Damon that she did it now without conscious effort. "Let's go home," she whispered. "There's nothing more we can do."

When they parted at Elena's door, Meredith said, "It's only two weeks until Founders' Day."

"I know." For a moment Damon's proposition swam in Elena's mind. But she shook her head to clear it. "I'll think of something," she said.

She hadn't thought of anything by the next day of school. The one encouraging fact was that Caroline didn't seem to have noticed anything amiss in her room – but that was *all* Elena could find to be encouraged about. There was an assembly that morning, at which it was announced that the school board had chosen Elena as the student to represent "The Spirit of Fell's Church". All through the principal's speech about it, Caroline's smile had blazed forth, triumphant and malicious.

Elena tried to ignore it. She did her best to ignore the slights and snubs that came even in the wake of the assembly, but it wasn't easy. It was never easy, and there were days when she thought she would hit someone or just start screaming, but so far she'd managed.

That afternoon, waiting for the sixth-period history class to be let out, Elena studied Tyler Smallwood. Since coming back to school, he had not addressed one word to her directly. He'd smiled as nastily as Caroline during the principal's announcement. Now, as he caught sight of Elena standing alone, he jostled Dick Carter with his elbow.

"What's that there?" he said. "A wallflower?"

Stefan, where are you? thought Elena. But she knew the answer to that. Halfway across school, in astronomy class.

Dick opened his mouth to say something, but then his expression changed. He was looking beyond Elena, down the hall. Elena turned and saw Vickie.

Vickie and Dick had been together before the Homecoming Dance. Elena supposed they still were. But Dick looked uncertain, as if he wasn't sure what to expect from the girl who was moving towards him.

There was something odd about Vickie's face, about her walk. She was moving as if her feet didn't touch the floor. Her eyes were dilated and dreamy.

"Hi there," Dick said tentatively, and he stepped in front of her. Vickie passed him without a glance and went on to Tyler. Elena watched what happened next with growing uneasiness. It should have been funny, but it wasn't.

It started with Tyler looking somewhat taken aback. Then Vickie put a hand on his chest. Tyler smiled, but there was a forced look about it. Vickie slid her hand under his jacket. Tyler's smile wavered. Vickie put her other hand on his chest. Tyler looked at Dick.

"Hey, Vickie, lighten up," said Dick hastily, but he didn't move any closer.

Vickie slid her two hands upwards, pushing Tyler's jacket off his shoulders. He tried to shrug it back on without letting go of his books or seeming too concerned. He couldn't. Vickie's fingers crept under his shirt.

"Stop that. Stop her, will you?" said Tyler to Dick. He had backed up against the wall.

"Hey, Vickie, leggo. Don't do that." But Dick remained at a safe distance. Tyler shot him an enraged glare and tried to shove Vickie away.

A noise had begun. At first it seemed to be at a frequency almost too low for human hearing, but it grew louder and louder. A growl, eerily menacing, that sent ice down Elena's spine. Tyler was looking pop-eyed with disbelief, and she soon realised why. The sound was coming from Vickie.

Then everything happened at once. Tyler was on the ground with Vickie's teeth snapping centimetres from his throat. Elena, all quarrels forgotten, was trying to help Dick pull her off. Tyler was howling. The history room door was open and Alaric was shouting.

"Don't hurt her! Be careful! It's epilepsy, we just need to get her lying down!"

Vickie's teeth snapped again as he reached a helpful hand into the melee. The slender girl was stronger than all of them put together, and they were losing control of her. They weren't going to be able to hold her for much longer. It was with intense relief that Elena heard a familiar voice at her shoulder.

"Vickie, calm down. It's all right. Just relax now."

With Stefan grasping Vickie's arm and talking to her soothingly, Elena dared to slacken her own grip. And it seemed, at first, that Stefan's strategy was working. Vickie's clawing fingers loosened, and they were able to lift her off Tyler. As Stefan kept speaking to her, she went limp and her eyes shut.

"That's good. You're feeling tired now. It's all right to go to sleep."

But then, abruptly, it stopped working, and whatever Power Stefan had been exercising over her was broken. Vickie's eyes flew open, and they bore no resemblance to the startled fawn's eyes Elena had seen in the cafeteria. They were blazing with red fury. She snarled at Stefan and burst out fighting with fresh strength.

It took five or six of them to hold her down while somebody called the police. Elena stayed where she was, talking to Vickie, sometimes yelling at her, until the police got there. None of it did any good.

Then she stepped back and saw the crowd of onlookers for the first time. Bonnie was in the front row, staring open-mouthed. So was Caroline.

"What *happened*?" said Bonnie as the officials carried Vickie away.

Elena, panting gently, pushed a strand of hair out of her eyes. "She went crazy and tried to undress Tyler."

Bonnie pursed her lips. "Well, she'd have to be crazy to *want* to, wouldn't she?" And she threw a smirk over her shoulder directly at Caroline.

Elena's knees were rubbery and her hands were shaking. She felt an arm go around her, and she leaned against Stefan gratefully. Then she looked up at him.

"Epilepsy?" she said with disbelieving scorn.

He was gazing down the hall after Vickie. Alaric Saltzman, still shouting instructions, was apparently going with her. The group turned the corner.

"I think class was just dismissed," Stefan said. "Let's go."

They walked towards the boarding house in silence, each lost in thought. Elena frowned, and several times glanced over at Stefan, but it wasn't until they were alone in his room that she spoke.

"Stefan, what is all this? What's happening to Vickie?"

"That's what I've been wondering. There's only one explanation I can think of, and it's that she's still under attack."

"You mean Damon's still – oh, my God! Oh, Stefan, I should have given her some of the vervain. I should have realised . . ."

"It wouldn't have made any difference. Believe me." She had turned towards the door as if to go after Vickie that minute, but he pulled her gently back. "Some people are more easily influenced than others, Elena. Vickie's will was never very strong. It belongs to him, now."

Slowly, Elena sat down. "Then there's nothing anyone can do? But, Stefan, will she become – like you and Damon?"

"It depends." His tone was bleak. "It's not just a matter of how much blood she loses. She needs *his* blood in her veins to make the change complete. Otherwise, she'll just end up like Mr Tanner. Drained, used up. Dead."

Elena took a long breath. There was something else she wanted to ask him about, something she'd wanted to ask him for a long time. "Stefan, when you spoke to Vickie back there, I thought it was working. You were using your Powers on her, weren't you?"

"Yes."

"But then she just went crazy again. What I mean is . . . Stefan, you *are* OK, aren't you? Your Powers have come back?"

He didn't answer. But that was answer enough for her. "Stefan, why didn't you tell me? What's wrong?" She went around and knelt by him so that he had to look at her.

"It's taking me a while to recover, that's all. Don't worry about it."

"I *am* worried. Isn't there anything we can do?"

"No," he said. But his eyes dropped.

Comprehension swept through Elena. "*Oh*," she whispered, sitting back. Then she reached for him again, trying to get hold of his hands. "Stefan, listen to me—"

"Elena, *no*. Don't you see? It's dangerous, dangerous for both of us, but especially for you. It could kill you, or worse."

"Only if you lose control," she said. "And you won't. Kiss me."

"*No*," said Stefan again. He added, less harshly, "I'll go out hunting tonight as soon as it's dark."

"Is that the same?" she said. She knew it wasn't. It was human blood that gave Power. "Oh, Stefan, please; don't you see I want to? Don't *you* want to?"

"That isn't fair," he said, his eyes tortured. "You know it isn't, Elena. You know how much –" He turned away from her again, his hands clenched into fists.

"Then why not? Stefan, I need . . ." She couldn't finish. She couldn't explain to him what she needed; it was a need for connection to him, for closeness. She needed to remember what it was like with him, to wipe out the memory of dancing in her dream and of Damon's arms locked around her. "I need us to be together again," she whispered.

Stefan was still turned away, and he shook his head.

"All right," Elena whispered, but she felt a wash of grief and fear as defeat seeped into her bones. Most of the fear was for Stefan, who was vulnerable without his Powers, vulnerable enough that he might be hurt by the ordinary citizens of Fell's Church. But some of it was for herself.

CHAPTER

A voice spoke as Elena reached for a can on the store shelf.

"Cranberry sauce already?"

Elena looked up. "Hi, Matt. Yes, Aunt Judith likes to do a preview the Sunday before Thanksgiving, remember? If she practises, there's less chance she'll do something terrible."

"Like forgetting to buy the cranberry sauce until fifteen minutes before dinner?"

"Until five minutes before dinner," said Elena, consulting her watch, and Matt laughed. It was a good sound, and one Elena hadn't heard for too long. She moved on toward the checkout, but after she'd paid for her purchase she hesitated, looking back. Matt was standing by the magazine rack, apparently absorbed, but there was something about the slope of his shoulders that made her want to go to him.

She poked a finger at his magazine. "What are *you* doing for dinner?" she said. When he glanced uncertainly towards the front of the store, she added, "Bonnie's waiting out in the car; she'll be there. Other than that it's just the family. And Robert, of course; he should be there by now." She meant that Stefan wasn't coming. She still wasn't sure how things were between Matt and Stefan these days. At least they spoke to each other.

"I'm fending for myself tonight; Mum's not feeling so hot," he said. But then, as if to change the subject, he went on, "Where's Meredith?"

"With her family, visiting some relatives or something." Elena was vague because Meredith had been vague herself; she seldom talked about her family. "So what do you think? Want to take a chance on Aunt Judith's cooking?"

"For old times' sake?"

"For old *friends'* sake," said Elena after a moment's hesitation, and smiled at him.

He blinked and looked away. "How can I refuse an invitation like that?" he said in an oddly muted voice. But when he put the magazine back and followed her out he was smiling, too.

Bonnie greeted him cheerfully, and when they got home Aunt Judith looked pleased to see him come into the kitchen.

"Dinner's almost ready," she said, taking the grocery bag from Elena. "Robert got here a few minutes ago. Why don't you go straight through to the dining room? Oh, and get another chair, Elena. Matt makes seven."

"Six, Aunt Judith," said Elena, amused. "You and Robert, me and Margaret, Matt and Bonnie."

"Yes, dear, but Robert's brought a guest, too. They're already sitting down."

Elena registered the words just as she stepped through the dining room door, but there was an instant's delay before her mind reacted to them. Even so, she *knew*; stepping through that door, she somehow knew what was waiting for her.

Robert was standing there, fiddling with a bottle of white wine and looking jovial. And sitting at the table, on the far side of the autumn centrepiece and the tall lighted candles, was Damon.

Elena realised she'd stopped moving when Bonnie ran into her from behind. Then she forced her legs into action. Her mind wasn't as obedient; it remained frozen.

"Ah, Elena," Robert said, holding out a hand. "This is Elena, the girl I was telling you about," he said to Damon. "Elena, this is Damon . . . ah . . ."

"Smith," said Damon.

"Oh, yes. He's from my college, William and Mary, and I just ran into him outside the chemist. Since he was looking for some place to eat, I invited him along here for a home-cooked meal. Damon, these are some friends of Elena's, Matt and Bonnie."

"Hi," said Matt. Bonnie just stared; then, she swung enormous eyes on Elena.

Elena was trying to get a grip on herself. She didn't

know whether to shriek, march out of the room, or throw the glass of wine Robert was pouring in Damon's face. She was too angry, for the moment, to be frightened.

Matt went to bring in a chair from the living room. Elena wondered at his casual acceptance of Damon, and then realised he hadn't been at Alaric's party. He wouldn't know what had happened there between Stefan and the "visitor from college".

Bonnie, though, looked ready to panic. She was gazing at Elena imploringly. Damon had risen and was holding out a chair for her.

Before Elena could come up with a response, she heard Margaret's high little voice in the doorway. "Matt, do you want to see my kitty? Aunt Judith says I can keep her. I'm going to call her Snowball."

Elena turned, fired with an idea.

"She's cute," Matt was saying obligingly, bending over the little mound of white fur in Margaret's arms. He looked startled as Elena unceremoniously grabbed the kitten from under his nose.

"Here, Margaret, let's show your kitty to Robert's friend," she said, and thrust the fluffy bundle into Damon's face, all but throwing it at him.

Pandemonium ensued. Snowball swelled to twice her normal size as her fur stood on end. She made a noise like water dropped on a red-hot griddle and then she was a snarling, spitting cyclone that clawed Elena, swiped at Damon, and ricocheted off the walls before tearing out of the room.

For an instant, Elena had the satisfaction of seeing

Damon's night-black eyes slightly wider than usual. Then the lids drooped down, hooding them again, and Elena turned to face the reaction of the other occupants of the room.

Margaret was just opening her mouth for a steam engine wail. Robert was trying to forestall it, hustling her off to find the cat. Bonnie had her back pressed flat against the wall, looking desperate. Matt and Aunt Judith, who was peering in from the kitchen, just looked appalled.

"I guess you don't have a way with animals," she said to Damon, and took her seat at the table. She nodded to Bonnie who reluctantly peeled herself off the wall and scuttled for her own seat before Damon could touch the chair. Bonnie's brown eyes slid around to follow him as he sat down in turn.

After a few minutes, Robert reappeared with a tear-stained Margaret and frowned sternly at Elena. Matt pushed his own chair in silently although his eyebrows were in his hair.

As Aunt Judith arrived and the meal began, Elena looked up and down the table. A bright haze seemed to lie over everything, and she had a feeling of unreality, but the scene itself looked almost unbelievably wholesome, like something out of a commercial. Just your average family sitting down to eat turkey, she thought. One slightly flustered aunt, worried that the peas will be mushy and the rolls burnt, one comfortable uncle-to-be, one golden-haired teenage niece and her baby sister. One blue-eyed boy-next-door type, one spritely girlfriend, one gorgeous vampire passing the vegetables. A typical American household.

Bonnie spent the first half of the meal telegraphing "What do I do?" messages to Elena with her eyes. But when all Elena telegraphed back was "Nothing", she apparently decided to abandon herself to her fate. She began to eat.

Elena had no idea what to do. To be trapped like this was an insult, a humiliation, and Damon knew it. He had Aunt Judith and Robert dazzled, though, with compliments about the meal and light chat about William and Mary. Even Margaret was smiling at him now, and soon enough Bonnie would go under.

"Fell's Church is having its Founders' Day celebration next week," Aunt Judith informed Damon, her thin cheeks faintly pink. "It would be so nice if you could come back for that."

"I'd like to," said Damon affably.

Aunt Judith looked pleased. "And this year Elena has a big part in it. She's been chosen to represent the Spirit of Fell's Church."

"You must be proud of her," said Damon.

"Oh, we are," Aunt Judith said. "So you'll try to come then?"

Elena broke in, buttering a roll furiously. "I've heard some news about Vickie," she said. "You remember, the girl who was attacked." She looked pointedly at Damon.

There was a short silence. Then Damon said, "I'm afraid I don't know her."

"Oh, I'm sure you do. About my height, brown eyes, light brown hair . . . anyway, she's getting worse."

"Oh, dear," said Aunt Judith.

"Yes, apparently the doctors can't understand it. She just keeps getting worse and worse, as if the attack was still going on." Elena kept her eyes on Damon's face as she spoke, but he displayed only a courteous interest. "Have some more stuffing," she finished, propelling a bowl at him.

"No, thank you. I'll have some more of this, though." He held a spoonful of cranberry sauce up to one of the candles so that light shone through it. "It's such a tantalising colour."

Bonnie, like the rest of the people at the table, looked up at the candle when he did this. But Elena noticed she didn't look down again. She remained gazing into the dancing flame, and slowly all expression disappeared from her face.

Oh, *no*, thought Elena, as a tingle of apprehension crept through her limbs. She'd seen that look before. She tried to get Bonnie's attention, but the other girl seemed to see nothing but the candle.

". . . and then the elementary children put on a pageant about the town's history," Aunt Judith was saying to Damon. "But the ending ceremony is done by older students. Elena, how many seniors will be doing the readings this year?"

"Just three of us." Elena had to turn to address her aunt, and it was while she was looking at Aunt Judith's smiling face that she heard the voice.

"Death."

Aunt Judith gasped. Robert paused with his fork halfway to his mouth. Elena wished, wildly and absolutely hopelessly, for Meredith.

"Death," said the voice again. "Death is in this house."

Elena looked around the table and saw that there was no one to help her. They were all staring at Bonnie, motionless as subjects in a photograph.

Bonnie herself was staring into the candle flame. Her face was blank, her eyes wide, as they had been before when this voice spoke through her. Now, those sightless eyes turned toward Elena. "Your death," the voice said. "Your death is waiting, Elena. It is—"

Bonnie seemed to choke. Then she pitched forwards and almost landed in her dinner plate.

There was an instant's paralysis, and then everyone moved. Robert jumped up and pulled at Bonnie's shoulders, lifting her. Bonnie's skin had gone bluish-white, her eyes were closed. Aunt Judith fluttered around her, dabbing at her face with a damp napkin. Damon watched with thoughtful, narrowed eyes.

"She's all right," Robert said, looking up in obvious relief. "I think she just fainted. It must have been some kind of hysterical attack." But Elena didn't breathe again until Bonnie opened groggy eyes and asked what everyone was staring at.

It put an effective end to the dinner. Robert insisted that Bonnie be taken home at once, and in the activity that followed Elena found time for a whispered word with Damon.

"Get out!"

He raised his eyebrows. "What?"

"I said, get out! Now! Go. Or I'll tell them you're the killer."

He looked reproachful. "Don't you think a guest deserves a little more consideration?" he said, but at her expression he shrugged and smiled.

"Thank you for having me for dinner," he said aloud to Aunt Judith, who was walking past carrying a blanket to the car. "I hope I can return the favour sometime." To Elena he added, "Be seeing you."

Well, *that* was clear enough, Elena thought, as Robert drove away with a sombre Matt and a sleepy Bonnie. Aunt Judith was on the phone with Mrs McCullough.

"I don't know what it is with these girls, either," she said. "First Vickie, now Bonnie . . . and Elena has not been herself lately . . ."

While Aunt Judith talked and Margaret searched for the missing Snowball, Elena paced.

She would have to call Stefan. That was all there was to it. She wasn't worried about Bonnie; the other times this had happened hadn't seemed to do permanent damage. And Damon would have better things to do than harass Elena's friends tonight.

He was coming here, to collect for the "favour" he'd done her. She knew without a doubt that that was the meaning of his final words. And it meant she would have to tell Stefan everything, because she needed him tonight, needed his protection.

Only, what could Stefan do? Despite all her pleas

and arguments last week, he had refused to take her blood. He'd insisted that his Powers would return without it, but Elena knew he was still vulnerable right now. Even if Stefan were here, could he stop Damon? Could he do it without being killed himself?

Bonnie's house was no refuge. And Meredith was gone. There was no one to help her, no one she could trust. But the thought of waiting here alone tonight, knowing that Damon was coming, was unbearable.

She heard Aunt Judith click down the receiver. Automatically, she moved towards the kitchen, Stefan's number running through her mind. Then she stopped, and slowly turned around to look at the living room she'd just left.

She looked at the floor to ceiling windows and at the elaborate fireplace with its beautifully scrolled moulding. This room was part of the original house, the one that had almost completely burned in the Civil War. Her own bedroom was just above.

A great light was beginning to dawn. Elena looked at the moulding around the ceiling, at where it joined the more modern dining room. Then she almost ran towards the stairs, her heart beating fast.

"Aunt Judith?" Her aunt paused on the stairway. "Aunt Judith, tell me something. Did Damon go into the living room?"

"What!" Aunt Judith blinked at her in distraction.

"Did Robert take Damon into the living room? Please think, Aunt Judith! I need to know."

"Why, no, I don't think so. No, he didn't. They came in and went straight to the dining room. Elena, what on earth . . . ?" This last as Elena impulsively threw her arms around her and hugged her.

"Sorry, Aunt Judith. I'm just happy," said Elena. Smiling, she turned to go back down the stairs.

"Well, I'm glad *someone's* happy, after the way dinner turned out. Although that nice boy, Damon, seemed to enjoy himself. Do you know, Elena, he seemed quite taken with you, in spite of the way you were acting."

Elena turned back around. "So?"

"Well, I just thought you might give him a chance, that's all. I thought he was very pleasant. The kind of young man I like to see around here."

Elena goggled for a moment, then swallowed to keep the hysterical laughter from escaping. Her aunt was suggesting that she take up Damon instead of Stefan . . . because Damon was safer. The kind of nice young man any aunt would like. "Aunt Judith," she began, gasping, but then she realised it was useless. She shook her head mutely, throwing her hands up in defeat, and watched her aunt go up the stairs.

Usually Elena slept with her door closed. But tonight she left it open and lay on her bed gazing out into the darkened hallway. Every so often she glanced at the luminous numbers of the clock on the bedside table beside her.

There was no danger that she would fall asleep. As the minutes crawled by, she almost began to wish she could. Time moved with agonising slowness. Eleven o'clock . . . eleven thirty . . . midnight. One a.m. One-thirty. Two.

At 2:10 she heard a sound.

She listened, still lying on her bed, to the faint whisper of noise downstairs. She'd known he would find a way to get in if he wanted. If Damon was that determined, no lock would keep him out.

Music from the dream she'd had that night at Bonnie's tinkled through her mind, a handful of plaintive, silvery notes. It woke strange feelings inside her. Almost in a daze or dream herself, she got up and went to stand at the threshold.

The hallway was dark, but her eyes had had a long time to adjust. She could see the darker silhouette making its way up the stairs. When it reached the top she saw the swift, deadly glimmer of his smile.

She waited, unsmiling, until he reached her and stood facing her, with only a yard of hardwood floor between them. The house was completely silent. Across the hall Margaret slept; at the end of the passage, Aunt Judith lay wrapped in dreams, unaware of what was going on outside her door.

Damon said nothing, but he looked at her, his eyes taking in the long white nightgown with its high, lacy neck. Elena had chosen it because it was the most modest one she owned, but Damon obviously thought it attractive. She forced herself to stand quietly, but her mouth was dry and her heart was thudding dully. Now was the time. In another minute she would know.

She backed up, without a word or gesture of

invitation, leaving the doorway empty. She saw the quick flare in his bottomless eyes, and watched him come eagerly towards her. And watched him stop.

He stood just outside her room, plainly disconcerted. He tried again to step forwards but could not. Something seemed to be preventing him from moving any further. On his face, surprise gave way to puzzlement and then anger.

He looked up, his eyes raking over the lintel, scanning the ceiling on either side of the threshold. Then, as the full realisation hit him, his lips pulled back from his teeth in an animal snarl.

Safe on her side of the doorway, Elena laughed softly. It had worked.

"My room and the living room below are all that's left of the old house," she said to him. "And, of course, that was a different dwelling place. One you were *not* invited into, and never will be."

His chest was heaving with anger, his nostrils dilated, his eyes wild. Waves of black rage emanated from him. He looked as if he would like to tear the walls down with his hands, which were twitching and clenching with fury.

Triumph and relief made Elena giddy. "You'd better go now," she said. "There's nothing for you here."

For one minute more those menacing eyes blazed into hers, and then Damon turned around. But he didn't head for the stairway. Instead, he took one step across the hall and laid his hand on the door to Margaret's room.

Elena started forwards before she knew what she

was doing. She stopped in the doorway, grasping the doorframe, her own breath coming hard.

His head whipped around and he smiled at her, a slow, cruel smile. He twisted the doorknob slightly without looking at it. His eyes, like pools of liquid ebony, remained on Elena.

"Your choice," he said.

Elena stood very still, feeling as if all of winter was inside her. Margaret was just a baby. He couldn't mean it; no one could be such a monster as to hurt a four-year-old.

But there was no hint of softness or compassion in Damon's face. He was a hunter, a killer, and the weak were his prey. She remembered the dreadful animal snarl that had transfigured his handsome features, and she knew that she could never leave Margaret to him.

Everything seemed to be happening in slow motion. She saw Damon's hand on the doorknob; she saw those merciless eyes. She was walking through the doorway, leaving behind the only safe place she knew.

Death was in the house, Bonnie had said. And now Elena had gone to meet Death of her own free will. She bowed her head to conceal the helpless tears that came to her eyes. It was over. Damon had won.

She did not look up to see him advance on her. But she felt the air stir around her, making her shiver. And then she was enfolded in soft, endless blackness, which wrapped around her like a great bird's wings.

CHAPTER

Elena stirred, then opened heavy eyelids. Light was showing around the edges of the curtains. She found it hard to move, so she lay there on her bed and tried to piece together what had happened last night.

Damon. Damon had come here and threatened Margaret. And so Elena had gone to him. He'd won.

But why hadn't he finished it? Elena lifted a languid hand to touch the side of her neck, already knowing what she would find. Yes, there they were: two small punctures that were tender and sensitive to pressure.

Yet she was still alive. He'd stopped short of carrying out his promise. Why?

Her memories of the last hours were confused and blurry. Only fragments were clear. Damon's eyes looking down at her, filling her whole world. The sharp sting at her throat. And, later, Damon opening his shirt, Damon's blood welling from a small cut in his neck.

He'd made her drink his blood then. If *made* was the right word. She didn't remember putting up any resistance or feeling any revulsion. By then, she had wanted it.

But she wasn't dead, or even seriously weakened. He hadn't made her into a vampire. And that was what she couldn't understand.

He has no morals and no conscience, she reminded herself. So it certainly wasn't mercy that stopped him. He probably just wants to draw the game out, make you suffer more before he kills you. Or maybe he wants you to be like Vickie, with one foot in the shadow world and one in the light. Going slowly mad that way.

One thing was sure: she wouldn't be fooled into thinking it was kindness on his part. Damon wasn't capable of kindness. Or of caring for anybody but himself.

Pushing the blankets back, she rose from the bed. She could hear Aunt Judith moving around in the hallway. It was Monday morning and she had to get ready to go to school.

27 November, Wednesday
Dear Diary,

It's no good pretending I'm not frightened, because I am. Tomorrow's Thanksgiving, and Founders' Day is two days after that. And I still haven't figured out a way to stop Caroline and Tyler.

I don't know what to do. If I can't get my diary back from Caroline, she's going to read it in front of everyone. She'll have a perfect opportunity; she's one of the three seniors chosen to read poetry during the closing ceremonies. Chosen by the school board, of which Tyler's father is a member, I might add. I wonder what he'll think when this is all over?

But what difference does it make? Unless I can come up with a plan, when this is all over I'll be beyond caring. And Stefan will be gone, run out of town by the good citizens of Fell's Church. Or dead, if he doesn't get some of his Powers back. And if he dies, I'll die too. It's that simple.

Which means I have to find a way to get the diary. I have to.

But I can't.

I know, you're waiting for me to say it. There is a way to get my diary – Damon's way. All I need to do is agree to his price.

But you don't understand how much that frightens me. Not just because Damon frightens me, but because I'm afraid of what will happen if he and I are together again. I'm afraid of what will happen to me . . . and to me and Stefan.

I can't talk about this any more. It's too upsetting. I feel so confused and lost and alone. There's nobody I can turn to or talk to. Nobody who could possibly understand.

What am I going to do?

28 November, Thursday, 11:30 p.m.
Dear Diary,

Things seem clearer today, maybe because I've come to a decision. It's a decision that terrifies me, but it's better than the only alternative I can think of.

I'm going to tell Stefan everything.

It's the only thing I can do now. Founders' Day is Saturday and I haven't come up with any plan of my own. But maybe Stefan can, if he realises how desperate the situation is. I'm going over to spend the day at the boarding house tomorrow, and when I get there I'm going to tell him everything I should have told him in the first place.

Everything. About Damon, too.

I don't know what he'll say. I keep remembering his face in my dreams. The way he looked at me, with such bitterness and anger. Not as if he loved me at all. If he looks at me like that tomorrow . . .

Oh, I'm scared. My stomach is churning. I could barely touch Thanksgiving dinner – and I can't keep still. I feel as if I might fly apart into a million pieces. Go to sleep tonight? Ha.

Please let Stefan understand. Please let him forgive me.

The funniest thing is, I wanted to become a better person for him. I wanted to be worthy of his love. Stefan has these ideas about honour, about what's right and wrong. And now, when he finds out how I've been lying to him, what will he think of me? Will he believe me, that I was only trying to protect him? Will he ever trust me again?

Tomorrow I'll know. Oh, God, I wish it were already over. I don't know how I'll live until then.

Elena slipped out of the house without telling Aunt Judith where she was going. She was tired of lies, but she didn't want to face the fuss there would inevitably be if she said she was going to Stefan's. Ever since Damon had come to dinner, Aunt Judith had been talking about him, throwing subtle and not-so-subtle hints into every conversation. And Robert was almost as bad. Elena sometimes thought he egged Aunt Judith on.

She leaned on the doorbell of the boarding house wearily. Where was Mrs Flowers these days? When the door finally opened, Stefan was behind it.

He was dressed for outdoors, his jacket collar turned up. "I thought we could go for a walk," he said.

"No." Elena was firm. She couldn't manage a real smile for him, so she stopped trying. She said, "Let's go upstairs, Stefan, all right? There's something we need to talk about."

He looked at her for a moment in surprise. Something must have shown in her face, for his expression gradually stilled and darkened. He took a deep breath and nodded. Without a word, he turned and led the way to his room.

The trunks and dressers and bookcases had long since been put back into order, of course. But Elena felt as if she was really noticing this for the first time. For some reason, she thought of the very first night she'd been here, when Stefan had saved her from Tyler's disgusting embrace. Her eyes ran over the objects on the dresser: the fifteenth-century gold florins, the ivory-hilted dagger, the little iron coffer with the hinged lid. She'd tried to open that the first night and he'd slammed the lid down.

She turned. Stefan was standing by the window, outlined by the rectangle of grey and dismal sky. Every day this week had been chilly and misty, and this was no exception. Stefan's expression mirrored the weather outside.

"Well," he said quietly, "what do we need to talk about?"

There was one last moment of choice, and then Elena committed herself. She stretched out a hand to the small iron coffer and opened it.

Inside, a length of apricot silk shone with muted lustre. Her hair ribbon. It reminded her of summer, of summer days that seemed impossibly far away just now. She gathered it up and held it out to Stefan.

"About this," she said.

He had taken a step forwards when she touched the coffer, but now he looked puzzled and surprised. "About *that*?"

"Yes. Because I knew it was there, Stefan. I found it a long time ago, one day when you left the room for a few minutes. I don't know why I had to know what was in there, but I couldn't help it. So I found the ribbon. And then . . ." She stopped and braced herself. "Then I wrote about it in my diary."

Stefan was looking more and more bewildered, as if this was not at all what he'd been expecting. Elena groped for the right words.

"I wrote about it because I thought it was evidence that you'd cared about me all along, enough to pick it up and keep it. I never thought it could be evidence of anything else."

Then, suddenly, she was speaking quickly. She told him about taking her diary to Bonnie's house, about how it had been stolen. She told him about getting the notes, about realising that Caroline was the one who was sending them. And then, turning away, pulling the summer-coloured silk over and over through her nervous fingers, she told him about Caroline and Tyler's plan.

Her voice almost gave out at the end. "I've been so frightened since then," she whispered, her eyes still on the ribbon. "Scared that you'd be angry with me. Scared of what they're going to do. Just scared. I tried to get the diary back, Stefan, I even went to Caroline's house. But she has it too well hidden. And I've thought and thought, but I can't think of any way of stopping her from reading it." At last she looked up at him. "I'm sorry."

"You should be!" he said, startling her with his vehemence. She felt the blood drain from her face. But Stefan was going on. "You should be sorry for keeping something like that from me when I could have helped you. Elena, why didn't you just *tell* me?"

"Because it's all my fault. And I had a dream . . ." She tried to describe how he had looked in the dreams, the bitterness, the accusation in his eyes. "I think I would die if you really looked at me that way," she concluded miserably.

But Stefan's expression as he looked at her now was a combination of relief and wonder. "So that's it," he said, almost in a whisper himself. "That's what's been bothering you."

Elena opened her mouth, but he was still speaking. "I knew something was wrong, I knew you were holding something back. But I thought . . ." He shook his head and a skewed smile tugged at his lips. "It doesn't matter now. I didn't want to invade your privacy. I didn't even want to ask. And all the time you were worried about protecting *me*."

Elena's tongue was stuck to the roof of her mouth. The words seemed to be stuck, too. There's more, she thought, but she couldn't say it, not when Stefan's eyes looked like that, not when his whole face was alight that way.

"When you said we needed to talk today, I thought you'd changed your mind about me," he said simply, without self-pity. "And I wouldn't have blamed you. But instead . . ." He shook his head again. "Elena," he said, and then she was in his arms.

It felt so good to be there, so *right*. She hadn't even realised how wrong things had been between them until now, when the wrongness had disappeared. *This* was what she remembered, what she had felt that first glorious night when Stefan had held her. All the sweetness and tenderness in the world surging between them. She was home, where she belonged. Where she would always belong.

Everything else was forgotten.

As she had in the beginning, Elena felt as if she could almost read Stefan's thoughts. They were connected, a part of each other. Their hearts beat to the same rhythm.

Only one thing was needed to make it complete. Elena knew that, and she tossed her hair back, reaching from behind to pull it away from the side of her neck. And this time Stefan did not protest or thwart her. Instead of refusal he was radiating a deep acceptance – and a deep need.

Feelings of love, of delight, of appreciation overwhelmed her and with incredulous joy she realised the feelings were his. For a moment, she sensed herself through his eyes, and sensed how much he cared for her. It might have been frightening if she had not had the same depth of feeling to give back to him.

She felt no pain as his teeth pierced her neck. And it didn't even occur to her that she had unthinkingly offered him the unmarked side – even though the wounds Damon had left were healed already.

She clung to him when he tried to lift his head. He was adamant, though, and at last she had to let him do it. Still holding her, he groped over on to the dresser for the wicked ivory-handled blade and with one quick motion he let his own blood flow.

When Elena's knees grew weak, he sat her on the bed. And then they just held each other, unaware of time or anything else. Elena felt that only she and Stefan existed.

"I love you," he said softly.

At first Elena, in her pleasant haze, simply accepted the words. Then, with a chill of sweetness, she realised what he'd said.

He loved her. She'd known it all along, but he had never said it before.

"I love you, Stefan," she whispered back. She was surprised when he shifted and pulled away slightly, until she saw what he was doing. Reaching inside his sweater, he drew out the chain he had worn around his neck ever since she had known him. On the chain was a gold ring, exquisitely crafted, set with lapis lazuli.

Katherine's ring. As Elena watched, he took the chain off and unclasped it, removing the delicate golden band.

"When Katherine died," he said, "I thought I could never love anyone else. Even though I knew she would have wanted me to, I was sure it could never happen. But I was wrong." He hesitated a moment and then went on.

"I kept the ring because it was a symbol of her. So I could keep her in my heart. But now I'd like it to be a symbol of something else." Again he hesitated, seeming almost afraid to meet her eyes. "Considering the way things are, I don't really have any right to ask this. But, Elena—" He struggled on for a few minutes and then gave up, his eyes meeting hers mutely.

Elena couldn't speak. She couldn't even breathe. But Stefan misinterpreted her silence. The hope in his eyes died and he turned away.

"You're right," he said. "It's all impossible. There are just too many difficulties – because of me. Because of what I am. Nobody like you should be tied to someone like me. I shouldn't even have suggested it—"

"Stefan!" said Elena. "Stefan, if you'll be quiet a moment—"

"—so just forget I said anything—"

"*Stefan!*" she said. "Stefan, *look at me*."

Slowly, he obeyed, turning back. He looked into her eyes, and the bitter self-condemnation faded from his face, to be replaced by a look that made her lose her breath again. Then, still slowly, he took the hand she was holding out. Deliberately, as they both watched, he slipped the ring on to her finger.

It fit as if it had been made for her. The gold glinted richly in the light, and the lapis shone a deep vibrant blue like a clear lake surrounded by untouched snow.

"We'll have to keep it a secret for a while," she said, hearing the tremor in her voice. "Aunt Judith will have a fit if she knows I'm engaged before I graduate. But I'll be eighteen next summer, and then she can't stop us."

"Elena, are you sure this is what you want? It won't be easy living with me. I'll always be different from you, no matter how I try. If you ever want to change your mind . . ."

"As long as you love me, I'll never change my mind."

He took her in his arms again, and peace and contentment enfolded her. But there was still one fear that gnawed at the edges of her consciousness.

"Stefan, about tomorrow – if Caroline and Tyler carry out their plan, it won't matter if I change my mind or not."

"Then we'll just have to make sure they can't carry it out. If Bonnie and Meredith will help me, I think I can find a way to get the diary from Caroline. But even if I can't, I'm not going to run. I won't leave you, Elena; I'm going to stay and fight."

"But they'll hurt you. Stefan, I can't stand that."

"And I can't leave you. That's settled. Let me worry about the rest of it; I'll find a way. And if I don't . . . well, no matter what I'll stay with you. We'll be together."

"We'll be together," Elena repeated, and rested her head on his shoulder, happy to stop thinking for a while and just *be*.

29 November, Friday

Dear Diary,

It's late but I couldn't sleep. I don't seem to need as much sleep as I used to.

Well, tomorrow's the day.

We talked to Bonnie and Meredith tonight. Stefan's plan is simplicity itself. The thing is, no matter where Caroline has hidden the diary, she has to bring it out tomorrow to take it with her. But our readings are the last thing on the agenda, and she has to be in the parade and everything first. She'll have to stash the diary somewhere during that time. So if we watch her from the minute she leaves her house until she gets up on stage, we should be able to see where she puts it down. And since she doesn't even know we're suspicious, she won't be on guard.

That's when we get it.

The reason the plan will work is because everyone concerned will be in period dress. Mrs Grimesby, the librarian, will help us put on our 19th-century clothes before the parade, and we can't be wearing or carrying anything that's not part of the costume. No purses, no backpacks. No diaries! Caroline will have to leave it behind at some point.

We're taking turns watching her. Bonnie is going to wait outside her house and see what Caroline's carrying when she leaves. I'll watch her when she gets dressed at Mrs Grimesby's house. Then, while the parade is going on, Stefan and Meredith will break into the house – or the Forbes' car, if that's where it is – and do their stuff.

I don't see how it can fail. And I can't tell you how much better I feel. It's so good just to be able to share this problem with Stefan. I've learned my lesson; I'll never keep things from him again.

I'm wearing my ring tomorrow. If Mrs Grimesby asks me about it, I'll tell her it's even older than 19th century, it's from Renaissance Italy. I'd like to see her face when I say that.

I'd better try to get some sleep now. I hope I don't dream.

CHAPTER

Bonnie shivered as she waited outside the tall Victorian house. The air was frosty this morning, and although it was almost eight o'clock the sun had never really come up. The sky was just one dense massed bank of grey and white clouds, creating an eerie twilight below.

She had begun to stamp her feet and rub her hands together when the Forbes' door opened. Bonnie moved back a little behind the shrubbery that was her hiding place and watched the family walk to their car. Mr Forbes was carrying nothing but a camera. Mrs Forbes had a purse and a folding seat. Daniel Forbes, Caroline's younger brother, had another seat. And Caroline . . .

Bonnie leaned forwards, her breath hissing out in satisfaction. Caroline was dressed in jeans and a heavy sweater, and she was carrying some sort of white drawstring purse. Not big but big enough to hold a small diary.

Warmed by triumph, Bonnie waited behind the bush until the car drove away. Then she started for the corner of Thrush Street and Hawthorne Drive.

"There she is, Aunt Judith. On the corner."

The car slowed to a halt, and Bonnie slid into the back seat with Elena.

"She's got a white drawstring purse," she murmured into Elena's ear as Aunt Judith pulled out again.

Tingling excitement swept over Elena, and she squeezed Bonnie's hand. "Good," she breathed. "Now we'll see if she brings it into Mrs Grimesby's. If not, you tell Meredith it's in the car."

Bonnie nodded agreement and squeezed Elena's hand back.

They arrived at Mrs Grimesby's just in time to see Caroline going inside with a white bag hanging from her arm. Bonnie and Elena exchanged a look. Now it was up to Elena to see where Caroline left it in the house.

"I'll get out here too, Miss Gilbert," said Bonnie as Elena jumped out of the car. She would wait outside with Meredith until Elena could tell them where the bag was. The important thing was not to let Caroline suspect anything unusual.

Mrs Grimesby, who answered Elena's knock, was the Fell's Church librarian. Her house looked almost like a library itself; there were bookcases everywhere and books stacked on the floor. She was also the keeper of Fell's Church's historical artifacts, including clothing that had been preserved from the town's earliest days.

Just now the house was ringing with young voices, and the bedrooms were full of students in various stages of undress. Mrs Grimesby always supervised the costumes for the pageant. Elena was ready to ask to be put in the same room as Caroline, but it wasn't necessary. Mrs Grimesby was already ushering her in.

Caroline, stripped down to her fashionable underwear, gave Elena what was undoubtedly meant to be a nonchalant look, but Elena detected the vicious gloating beneath. She kept her own eyes on the bundle of clothing Mrs Grimesby was picking up off the bed.

"Here you are, Elena. One of our most nicely preserved pieces – and all authentic, too, even the ribbons. We believe this dress belonged to Honoria Fell."

"It's beautiful," said Elena, as Mrs Grimesby shook out the folds of thin white material. "What's it made of?"

"Moravian muslin and silk gauze. Since it's quite cold today you can wear that velvet jacket over it." The librarian indicated a dusty rose garment lying over a chair back.

Elena cast a surreptitious glance at Caroline as she began to change. Yes, there was the bag, at Caroline's feet. She debated making a grab for it, but Mrs

Grimesby was still in the room.

The muslin dress was very simple, its flowing material belted high under the bosom with a pale rose ribbon. The slightly puffed elbow-length sleeves were tied with ribbon of the same colour. Fashions had been loose enough in the early nineteenth century to fit a twentieth-century girl – at least if she were slender. Elena smiled as Mrs Grimesby led her to a mirror.

"Did it really belong to Honoria Fell?" she asked, thinking of the marble image of that lady lying on her tomb in the ruined church.

"That's the story, anyway," said Mrs Grimesby. "She mentions a dress like it in her journal, so we're pretty sure."

"She kept a journal?" Elena was startled.

"Oh, yes. I have it in a case in the living room; I'll show it to you on the way out. Now for the jacket – oh, what's that?"

Something violet fluttered to the ground as Elena picked the jacket up.

She could feel her expression freeze. She caught up the note before Mrs Grimesby could bend over, and glanced at it.

One line. She remembered writing it in her diary on 4 September, the first day of school. Except that after she had written it she had crossed it out. These words were not crossed out; they were bold and clear.

Something awful is going to happen today.

Elena could barely restrain herself from rounding on Caroline and shaking the note in her face. But that would ruin everything. She forced herself to stay calm as she crumpled up the little slip of paper and threw it into a wastebasket.

"It's just a piece of rubbish," she said, and turned back to Mrs Grimesby, her shoulders stiff. Caroline said nothing, but Elena could feel those triumphant green eyes on her.

Just you wait, she thought. Wait until I get that diary back. I'm going to burn it, and then you and I are going to have a talk.

To Mrs Grimesby she said, "I'm ready."

"So am I," said Caroline in a demure voice. Elena put on a look of cool indifference as she eyed the other girl. Caroline's pale green gown with long green and white sashes was not nearly as pretty as hers.

"Wonderful. You girls go ahead and wait for your rides. Oh, and Caroline, don't forget your reticule."

"I won't," Caroline said, smiling, and she reached for the drawstring bag at her feet.

It was fortunate that from that position she couldn't see Elena's face, for in that instant the cool indifference shattered completely. Elena stared, dumbfounded, as Caroline began to tie the bag at her waist.

Her astonishment didn't escape Mrs Grimesby. "That's a reticule, the ancestor of our modern handbag," the older woman explained kindly. "Ladies used to keep their gloves and fans in them. Caroline came by and got it earlier this week so she could repair some loose beadwork ... very thoughtful of her."

"I'm sure it was," Elena managed in a strangled voice. She had to get out of here or something awful was going to happen right *now*. She was going to start screaming – or knock Caroline down – or explode. "I need some fresh air," she said. She bolted from the room and from the house, bursting outside.

Bonnie and Meredith were waiting in Meredith's car. Elena's heart thumped strangely as she walked to it and leaned in the window.

"She's outsmarted us," she said quietly. "That bag is part of her costume, and she's going to wear it all day."

Bonnie and Meredith stared, first at her and then at each other.

"But ... then, what are we going to do?" Bonnie asked.

"I don't know." With sick dismay this realisation finally came home to Elena. "I don't know!"

"We can still watch her. Maybe she'll take the bag off at lunch or something ..." But Meredith's voice rang hollow. They all knew the truth, Elena thought, and the truth was that it was hopeless. They'd lost.

Bonnie glanced in the rearview mirror, then twisted in her seat. "It's your ride."

Elena looked. Two white horses were drawing a smartly renovated buggy down the street. Crêpe paper was threaded through the buggy's wheels, ferns decorated its seats, and a large banner on the side proclaimed, *The Spirit of Fell's Church*.

Elena had time for only one desperate message. "Watch her," she said. "And if there's ever a moment when she's alone . . ." Then she had to go.

But all through that long, terrible morning, there was never a moment when Caroline was alone. She was surrounded by a crowd of spectators.

For Elena, the parade was pure torture. She sat in the buggy beside the mayor and his wife, trying to smile, trying to look normal. But the sick dread was like a crushing weight on her chest.

Somewhere in front of her, among the marching bands and drill teams and open convertibles, was Caroline. Elena had forgotten to find out which float she was on. The first schoolhouse float, perhaps; a lot of the younger children in costume would be on that.

It didn't matter. Wherever Caroline was, she was in full view of half the town.

The lunch that followed the parade was held in the high school cafeteria. Elena was trapped at a table with Mayor Dawley and his wife. Caroline was at a nearby table; Elena could see the shining back of her auburn head. And sitting beside her, often leaning possessively over her, was Tyler Smallwood.

Elena was in a perfect position to view the little drama that occurred about halfway through lunch. Her heart leaped into her throat when she saw Stefan, looking casual, stroll by Caroline's table.

He spoke to Caroline. Elena watched, forgetting even to play with the untouched food on her plate. But what she saw next made her heart plummet. Caroline tossed her head and replied to him briefly, and then turned back to her meal. And Tyler lumbered to his feet, his face reddening as he made an angry gesture. He didn't sit down again until Stefan turned away.

Stefan looked towards Elena as he left, and for a moment their eyes met in wordless communion.

There was nothing he could do, then. Even if his Powers had returned, Tyler was going to keep him away from Caroline. The crushing weight squeezed Elena's lungs so that she could scarcely breathe.

After that she simply sat in a daze of misery and despair until someone nudged her and told her it was time to go backstage.

She listened almost indifferently to Mayor Dawley's speech of welcome. He spoke about the "trying time" Fell's Church had faced recently, and about the community spirit that had sustained them these past months. Then awards were given out, for scholarship, for athletics, for community service. Matt came up to receive Outstanding Male Athlete of the Year, and Elena saw him look at her curiously.

Then came the pageant. The elementary school children giggled and tripped and forgot their lines as they portrayed scenes from the founding of Fell's Church through the Civil War. Elena watched them without taking any of it in. Ever since last night she'd been slightly dizzy and shaky, and now she felt as if she were coming down with the flu. Her brain, usually so full of schemes and calculations, was empty. She couldn't think any more. She almost couldn't care.

The pageant ended to popping flashbulbs and

tumultuous applause. When the last little Confederate soldier was off the stage, Mayor Dawley called for silence.

"And now," he said, "for the students who will perform the closing ceremonies. Please show your appreciation for the Spirit of Independence, the Spirit of Fidelity, and the Spirit of Fell's Church!"

The applause was even more thunderous. Elena stood beside John Clifford, the brainy senior who'd been chosen to represent the Spirit of Independence. On the other side of John was Caroline. In a detached, nearly apathetic way Elena noticed that Caroline looked magnificent: her head tilted back, her eyes blazing, her cheeks flushed with colour.

John went first, adjusting his glasses and the microphone before he read from the heavy brown book on the lectern. Officially, the seniors were free to choose their own selections; in practice they almost always read from the works of M C Marsh, the only poet Fell's Church had ever produced.

All through John's reading, Caroline was upstaging him. She smiled at the audience; she shook out her hair; she weighed the reticule hanging from her waist. Her fingers stroked the drawstring bag lovingly, and Elena found herself staring at it, hypnotised, memorising every bead.

John took a bow and resumed his place by Elena. Caroline threw her shoulders back and did a model's walk to the lectern.

This time the applause was mixed with whistles. But Caroline didn't smile; she had assumed an air of tragic responsibility. With exquisite timing she waited until the cafeteria was perfectly quiet to speak.

"I was planning to read a poem by M C Marsh today," she said, then, into the attentive stillness, "but I'm not going to. Why read from *this*—" She held up the nineteenth-century volume of poetry. "—when there is something much more . . . relevant . . . in a book I happened to find?"

Happened to steal, you mean, thought Elena. Her eyes sought among the faces in the crowd, and she located Stefan. He was standing towards the back, with Bonnie and Meredith stationed on either side as if protecting him. Then Elena noticed something else. Tyler, with Dick and several other guys, was standing just a few yards behind. The guys were older than high school age, and they looked tough, and there were five of them.

Go, thought Elena, finding Stefan's eyes again. She willed him to understand what she was saying. Go, Stefan; please leave before it happens. Go *now*.

Very slightly, almost imperceptibly, Stefan shook his head.

Caroline's fingers were dipping into the bag as if she just couldn't wait. "What I'm going to read is about Fell's Church *today*, not a hundred or two hundred years ago," she was saying, working herself up into a sort of exultant fever. "It's important *now*, because it's about somebody who's living in town with us. In fact he's right here in this room."

Tyler must have written the speech for her, Elena decided. Last month, in the gym, he'd shown quite a gift for that kind of thing. Oh, Stefan, oh, Stefan, I'm scared . . . Her thoughts jumbled into incoherence as Caroline plunged her hand into the bag.

"I think you'll understand what I mean when you hear it," Caroline said, and with a quick motion she pulled a velvet-covered book from the reticule and held it up dramatically. "I think it will explain a lot of what's been going on in Fell's Church recently." Breathing quickly and lightly, she looked from the spellbound audience to the book in her hand.

Elena had almost lost consciousness when Caroline jerked the diary out. Bright sparkles ran along the edges of her vision. The dizziness roared up, ready to overwhelm Elena, and then she noticed something.

It must be her eyes. The stage lights and flashbulbs must have dazzled them. She certainly felt ready to faint any minute; it was hardly surprising that she couldn't see properly.

The book in Caroline's hands looked *green*, not blue.

I must be going crazy . . . or this is a dream . . . or maybe it's a trick of the lighting. But look at Caroline's face!

Caroline, mouth working, was staring at the velvet book. She seemed to have forgotten the audience altogether. She turned the diary over and over in her hands, looking at all sides of it. Her movements became frantic. She thrust a hand into the reticule as if she somehow hoped to find something else in it. Then she cast a wild glance around the stage as if what she was looking for might have fallen to the ground.

The audience was murmuring, getting impatient. Mayor Dawley and the high school principal were exchanging tight-lipped frowns.

Having found nothing on the floor, Caroline was staring at the small book again. But now she was gazing at it as if it were a scorpion. With a sudden gesture, she wrenched it open and looked inside, as if her last hope was that only the cover had changed and the words inside might be Elena's.

Then she slowly looked up from the book at the packed cafeteria.

Silence had descended again, and the moment drew out, while every eye remained fixed on the girl in the pale green gown. Then, with an inarticulate sound, Caroline whirled and clattered off the stage. She struck at Elena as she went by, her face a mask of rage and hatred.

Gently, with a feeling of floating, Elena stooped to pick up what Caroline had tried to hit her with.

Caroline's diary.

There was activity behind Elena as people ran after Caroline, and in front of her as the audience exploded into comment, argument, discussion. Elena found Stefan. He looked as if jubilation was sneaking up on him. But he also looked as bewildered as Elena felt. Bonnie and Meredith were the same. As Stefan's gaze crossed hers, Elena felt a rush of gratitude and joy, but her predominant emotion was awe.

It was a miracle. Beyond all hope, they had been rescued. They'd been saved.

And then her eyes picked out another dark head among the crowd.

Damon was leaning . . . no, lounging . . . against the north wall. His lips were curved into a half smile, and his eyes met Elena's boldly.

Mayor Dawley was beside her, urging her forwards, quieting the crowd, trying to restore order. It was no use. Elena read her selection in a dreamy voice to a babbling group of people who weren't paying attention in the slightest. She wasn't paying attention, either; she had no idea what words she was saying. Every so often she looked at Damon.

There was applause, scattered and distracted, when she finished, and the mayor announced the rest of the events for that afternoon. And then it was all over, and Elena was free to go.

She floated offstage without any conscious idea of *where* she was going, but her legs carried her to the north wall. Damon's dark head moved out the side door and she followed it.

The air in the courtyard seemed deliciously cool after the crowded room, and the clouds above were silvery and swirling. Damon was waiting for her.

Her steps slowed but did not stop. She moved until she was only a foot or so away from him, her eyes searching his face.

There was a long moment of silence and then she spoke. "Why?"

"I thought you'd be more interested in *how*." He patted his jacket significantly. "I got invited in for coffee this morning after scraping up an acquaintance last week."

"But *why*?"

He shrugged, and for just an instant something like consternation flickered across his finely drawn features. It seemed to Elena that he himself didn't know why – or didn't want to admit it.

"For my own purposes," he said.

"I don't think so." Something was building between them, something that frightened Elena with its power. "I don't think that's the reason at all."

There was a dangerous glimmer in those dark eyes. "Don't push me, Elena."

She moved closer, so that she was almost touching him, and looked at him. "I think," she said, "that maybe you need to be pushed."

His face was only centimetres away from hers, and Elena never knew what might have happened if at that moment a voice hadn't broken in on them.

"You *did* manage to make it after all! I'm so glad!"

It was Aunt Judith. Elena felt as if she were being whisked from one world to another. She blinked dizzily, stepping back, letting out a breath she hadn't realised she was holding.

"And so you got to hear Elena read," Aunt Judith continued happily. "You did a beautiful job, Elena, but I don't know what was going on with Caroline. The girls in this town are all acting bewitched lately."

"Nerves," suggested Damon, his face carefully solemn. Elena felt an urge to giggle and then a wave of irritation. It was all very well to be grateful to Damon for saving them, but if not for Damon there wouldn't have been a problem in the first place. Damon had committed the crimes Caroline wanted to pin on Stefan.

"And where *is* Stefan?" she said, voicing her next thought aloud. She could see Bonnie and Meredith in the courtyard alone.

Aunt Judith's face showed her disapproval. "I haven't seen him," she said briefly. Then she smiled fondly. "But I have an idea; why don't you come to dinner with us, Damon? Then afterwards perhaps you and Elena could—"

"Stop it!" said Elena to Damon. He looked politely inquiring.

"What?" said Aunt Judith.

"Stop it!" Elena said to Damon again. "You know what. Just stop it right now!"

CHAPTER

15

"Elena, you're being rude!" Aunt Judith seldom got angry but she was angry now. "You're too old for this kind of behaviour."

"It's not rudeness! You don't understand—"

"I understand perfectly. You're acting just the way you did when Damon came to dinner. Don't you think a guest deserves a little more consideration?"

Frustration flooded over Elena. "You don't even know what you're talking about," she said. This was too much. To hear Damon's words coming from Aunt Judith's lips . . . it was unbearable.

"Elena!" A mottled flush was creeping up Aunt Judith's cheeks. "I'm *shocked* at you! And I *have* to say that this childish behaviour only started since you've been going out with that boy."

"Oh, 'that boy'." Elena glared at Damon.

"Yes, that boy!" Aunt Judith answered. "Ever since you lost your head over him you've been a different person. Irresponsible, secretive – and defiant! He's been a bad influence from the start, and I won't tolerate it any more."

"Oh, really?" Elena felt as if she were talking to Damon and Aunt Judith at once, and she looked back and forth between the two of them. All the emotions she'd been suppressing for the last days – for the last weeks, for the months since Stefan had come into her life – were surging forward. It was like a great tidal wave inside her, over which she had no control.

She realised she was shaking. "Well, that's too bad because you're going to have to tolerate it. I am *never* going to give Stefan up, not for anyone. Certainly not for *you*!" This last was meant for Damon, but Aunt Judith gasped.

"That's enough!" Robert snapped. He'd appeared with Margaret, and his face was dark. "Young lady, if this is how that boy encourages you to speak to your aunt—"

"He's not 'that boy'!" Elena took another step back, so she could face all of them. She was making a spectacle of herself, everyone in the courtyard was looking. But she didn't care. She had been keeping a lid on her feelings for so long, shoving down all the anxiety and the fear and the anger where it wouldn't be seen. All the worry about Stefan, all the terror over Damon, all the shame and humiliation she'd suffered at school, she'd buried it deep. But now it was coming back. All of it, all at once, in a maelstrom of impossible violence. Her heart was pounding crazily; her ears rang. She felt that nothing mattered except to hurt the people who stood in front of her, to show them all.

"He's not 'that boy'," she said again, her voice deadly cold. "He's Stefan and he's all I care about. And I happen to be engaged to him."

"Oh, don't be ridiculous!" Robert thundered. It was the last straw.

"Is this ridiculous?" She held up her hand, the ring towards them. "We're going to get married!"

"You are *not* going to get married," Robert began. Everyone was furious. Damon grabbed her hand and stared at the ring, then turned abruptly and strode away, every step full of barely leashed savagery. Robert was spluttering on in exasperation. Aunt Judith was fuming.

"Elena, I absolutely forbid you—"

"You're not my mother!" Elena cried. Tears were trying to force themselves out of her eyes. She needed to get away, to be alone, to be with someone who loved her. "If Stefan asks, tell him I'll be at the boarding house!" she added, and broke away through the crowd.

She half expected Bonnie or Meredith to follow her, but she was glad they didn't. The car park was full of cars but almost empty of people. Most of the families were staying for the afternoon activities. But a battered Ford sedan was parked nearby, and a familiar figure was unlocking the door.

"Matt! Are you leaving?" She made her decision

instantly. It was too cold to walk all the way to the boarding house.

"Huh? No, I've got to help Coach Lyman take the tables down. I was just putting this away." He tossed the Outstanding Athlete placard into the front seat. "Hey, are you OK?" His eyes widened at the sight of her face.

"Yes – no. I will be if I can get out of here. Look, can I take your car? Just for a little while?"

"Well . . . sure, but . . . I know, why don't you let me drive you? I'll go tell Coach Lyman."

"No! I just want to be alone . . . Oh, please don't ask any questions." She almost snatched the keys out of his hand. "I'll bring it back soon, I promise. Or Stefan will. If you see Stefan, tell him I'm at the boarding house. And thanks." She slammed the door on his protests and revved the engine, pulling out with a clash of gears because she wasn't used to the manual gears. She left him standing there staring after her.

She drove without really seeing or hearing anything outside, crying, locked in her own spinning tornado of emotions. She and Stefan would run away . . . They would elope . . . They would show everyone. She would never set foot in Fell's Church again.

And then Aunt Judith would be sorry. Then Robert would see how wrong he'd been. But Elena would never forgive them. Never.

As for Elena herself, she didn't need anybody. She certainly didn't need stupid old Robert E Lee, where you could go from being mega-popular to being a social pariah in one day just for loving the wrong person. She didn't need any family, or any friends, either . . .

Slowing down to cruise up the winding driveway of the boarding house, Elena felt her thoughts slow down, too.

Well . . . she wasn't mad at all of her friends. Bonnie and Meredith hadn't done anything. Or Matt. Matt was all right. In fact, she might not need him but his car had come in pretty handy.

In spite of herself Elena felt a strangled giggle well up in her throat. Poor Matt. People always borrowing his clunking dinosaur of a car. He must think she and Stefan were nuts.

The giggle let loose a few more tears and she sat and wiped them off, shaking her head. Oh, God, how did things turn out this way? What a day. She should be having a victory celebration because they'd beaten Caroline, and instead she was crying alone in Matt's car.

Caroline *had* looked pretty damn funny, though. Elena's body shook gently with slightly hysterical chuckles. Oh, the look on her face. Somebody had better have a video of that.

At last the sobs and giggles both abated and Elena felt a wash of tiredness. She leaned against the steering wheel trying not to think of anything for a while, and then she got out of the car.

She'd go and wait for Stefan, and then they'd both go back and deal with the mess she'd made. It would take a lot of cleaning up, she thought wearily. Poor

Aunt Judith. Elena had yelled at her in front of half the town.

Why had she let herself get so upset? But her emotions were still close to the surface, as she found when the boarding house door was locked and no one answered the bell.

Wonderful, she thought, her eyes stinging again. Mrs Flowers had gone off to the Founders' Day celebration, too. And now Elena had the choice of sitting in the car or standing out here in this windstorm . . .

It was the first time she'd noticed the weather, but when she did she looked around in alarm. The day had started out cloudy and chilly, but now there was a mist flowing along the ground, as if breathed out from the surrounding fields. The clouds were not just swirling, they were seething. And the wind was getting stronger.

It moaned through the branches of the oak trees, tearing off the remaining leaves and sending them down in showers. The sound was rising steadily now, not just a moan but a howl.

And there was something else. Something that came not just from the wind, but from the air itself, or the space around the air. A feeling of pressure, of menace, of some unimaginable force. It was gathering power, drawing nearer, closing in.

Elena spun to face the oak trees.

There was a group of them behind the house, and more beyond, blending into the forest. And beyond that were the river and the graveyard.

Something . . . was out there. Something . . . very bad . . .

"No," whispered Elena. She couldn't see it, but she could feel it, like some great shape rearing up to stand over her, blotting out the sky. She *felt* the evil, the hatred, the animal fury.

Bloodlust. Stefan had used the word, but she hadn't understood it. Now she felt this bloodlust . . . focused on her.

"No!"

Higher and higher, it was towering over her. She could still see nothing, but it was as if great wings unfolded, stretching to touch the horizon on either side. Something with a Power beyond comprehension . . . and it wanted to *kill* . . .

"*No!*" She ran for the car just as it stooped and dived for her. Her hands scrabbled at the door handle, and she fumbled frantically with the keys. The wind was screaming, shrieking, tearing at her hair. Gritty ice sprayed into her eyes, blinding her, but then the key turned and she jerked the door open.

Safe! She slammed the door shut again and brought her fist down on the lock. Then she flung herself across the seat to check the locks on the other side.

The wind roared with a thousand voices outside. The car began rocking.

"Stop it! Damon, stop it!" Her thin cry was lost in the cacophony. She put her hands out on the dashboard as if to balance the car and it rocked harder, ice pelting against it.

Then she saw something. The rear window was

clouding up, but she could discern the shape through it. It looked like some great bird made of mist or snow, but the outlines were hazy. All she was sure of was that it had huge sweeping wings . . . and that it was coming for her.

Get the key in the ignition. Get it in! Now go! Her mind was rapping orders at her. The ancient Ford wheezed and the tyres screamed louder than the wind as she took off. And the shape behind her followed, getting larger and larger in the rearview mirror.

Get to town, get to Stefan! Go! Go! But as she squealed on to Old Creek Road, turning left, the wheels locking, a bolt of lightning split the sky.

If she hadn't been skidding and braking already, the tree would have crashed down on her. As it was, the violent impact shook the car like an earthquake missing the front right fender by inches. The tree was a mass of heaving, pitching branches, its trunk blocking the way back to town completely.

She was trapped. Her only route home cut off. She was alone, there was no escape from this terrible Power . . .

Power. That was it; that was the key. "The stronger your Powers are, the more the rules of the dark bind you."

Running water!

Throwing the car into reverse, she brought it around and then slammed it forwards. The white shape banked and swooped, missing her as narrowly as the tree had, and then she was speeding down Old Creek Road into the worst of the storm.

It was still after her. Only one thought pounded in Elena's brain now. She had to cross running water, to leave this thing behind.

There were more cracks of lightning, and she glimpsed other trees falling, but she swerved around them. It couldn't be far now. She could see the river flickering past on her left side through the driving ice storm. Then she saw the bridge.

It was there; she'd made it! A gust threw sleet across the windshield, but with the wipers' next stroke she saw it fleetingly again. This was it, the turn should be about *here*.

The car lurched and skidded on to the wooden structure. Elena felt the wheels grip at slick planks and then felt them lock. Desperately, she tried to turn with the skid, but she couldn't see and there was no room . . .

And then she was crashing through the railing, the rotted wood of the footbridge giving way under weight it could no longer support. There was a sickening feeling of spinning, dropping, and the car hit the water.

Elena heard screams, but they didn't seem to be connected with her. The river welled up around her and everything was noise and confusion and pain. A window shattered as it was struck by debris, and then another. Dark water gushed across her, along with glass like ice. She was engulfed. She couldn't see; she couldn't get out.

And she couldn't breathe. She was lost in this hellish tumult, and there was no air. *She had to breathe.* She had to get out of here . . .

"Stefan, help me!" she screamed.

But her scream made no sound. Instead, the icy water rushed into her lungs, invading her. She thrashed against it, but it was too strong for her. Her struggles became wilder, more uncoordinated, and then they stopped.

Then everything was still.

Bonnie and Meredith were hunting around the perimeter of the school impatiently. They'd seen Stefan go this way, more or less coerced by Tyler and his new friends. They'd started to follow him, but then that business with Elena had started. And then Matt had informed them that she'd taken off. So they'd set out after Stefan again, but nobody was out here. There weren't even any buildings except one lonely hut.

"And now there's a storm coming!" Meredith said. "Listen to that wind! I think it's going to rain."

"Or snow!" Bonnie shuddered. "Where did they *go*?"

"I don't care; I just want to get under a roof. Here it comes!" Meredith gasped as the first sheet of icy rain hit her, and she and Bonnie ran for the nearest shelter – the hut.

And it was there that they found Stefan. The door was ajar, and when Bonnie looked in she recoiled.

"Tyler's goon squad!" she hissed. "Look out!"

Stefan had a semicircle of guys between him and the door. Caroline was in the corner.

"He must have it! He took it somehow; I know he did!" she was saying.

"Took what?" said Meredith, loudly. Everyone turned their way.

Caroline's face contorted as she saw them in the doorway and Tyler snarled. "Get out," he said. "You don't want to be involved in this."

Meredith ignored him. "Stefan, can I talk to you?"

"In a minute. Are you going to answer her question? Took what?" Stefan was concentrating on Tyler, totally focused.

"Sure, I'll answer her question. Right after I answer yours." Tyler's beefy hand thumped into his fist and he stepped forwards. "You're going to be dog meat, Salvatore."

Several of the tough guys sniggered.

Bonnie opened her mouth to say, "Let's get *out* of here." But what she actually said was, "The bridge."

It was weird enough to make everyone look at her.

"What?" said Stefan.

"The bridge," said Bonnie again, without meaning to say it. Her eyes bulged, alarmed. She could hear the voice coming from her throat, but she had no control over it. And then she felt her eyes go wider and her mouth drop open and she had her own voice back. "The bridge, oh, my God, the bridge! That's where Elena is! Stefan, we've got to save her. . . . Oh, hurry!"

"Bonnie, are you sure?"

"Yes, oh, God . . . that's where she's gone. She's drowning! *Hurry*!" Waves of thick blackness broke over Bonnie. But she couldn't faint now; they had to get to Elena.

Stefan and Meredith hesitated one minute, and then Stefan was through the goon squad, brushing them aside like tissue paper. They sprinted through the field towards the parking lot, dragging Bonnie behind. Tyler started after them, but stopped when the full force of the wind hit him.

"Why would she go out in this storm?" Stefan shouted as they sprang into Meredith's car.

"She was upset; Matt said she took off in his car," Meredith gasped back in the comparative quiet of the interior. She pulled out fast and turned into the wind, speeding dangerously. "She said she was going to the boarding house."

"No, she's at the bridge! Meredith, drive faster! Oh, God, we're going to be too late!" Tears were running down Bonnie's face.

Meredith floored it. The car swayed, buffeted by wind and sleet. All through that nightmare ride Bonnie sobbed, her fingers clutching the seat in front of her.

Stefan's sharp warning kept Meredith from running into the tree. They piled out and were immediately lashed and punished by the wind.

"It's too big to move! We'll have to walk," Stefan shouted.

Of course it was too big to move, Bonnie thought, already scrambling through the branches. It was a full-grown oak tree. But once on the other side, the icy gale whipped all thought out of her head.

Within minutes she was numb, and the road seemed to go on for hours. They tried to run but the wind beat them back. They could scarcely see; if it hadn't been for Stefan, they would have gone over the riverbank. Bonnie began to weave drunkenly. She was ready to fall to the ground when she heard Stefan shouting up ahead.

Meredith's arm around her tightened, and they broke again into a stumbling run. But as they neared the bridge what they saw brought them to a halt.

"Oh, my God . . . Elena!" screamed Bonnie. Wickery Bridge was a mass of splintered rubble. The railing on one side was gone and the planking had given way as if a giant fist had smashed it. Beneath, the dark water churned over a sickening pile of debris. Part of the debris, entirely underwater except for the headlights, was Matt's car.

Meredith was screaming, too, but she was screaming at Stefan. "No! You can't go down there!"

He never even glanced back. He dived from the bank, and the water closed over his head.

Later, Bonnie's memory of the next hour would be mercifully dim. She remembered waiting for Stefan while the storm raged endlessly on. She remembered that she was almost beyond caring by the time a hunched figure lurched out of the water. She remembered feeling no disappointment, only a vast and yawning grief, as she saw the limp thing Stefan laid out on the road.

And she remembered Stefan's face.

She remembered how he looked as they tried to do

something for Elena. Only that wasn't really Elena lying there, that was a wax doll with Elena's features. It was nothing that had ever been alive and it certainly wasn't alive now. Bonnie thought it seemed silly to go on poking and prodding at it like this, trying to get water out of its lungs and so on. Wax dolls didn't breathe.

She remembered Stefan's face when he finally gave up. When Meredith wrestled with him and yelled at him, saying something about over an hour without air, and brain damage. The words filtered in to Bonnie, but their meaning didn't. She just thought it odd that while Meredith and Stefan were screaming at each other they were both crying.

Stefan stopped crying after that. He just sat there holding the Elena-doll. Meredith yelled some more, but he didn't listen to her. He just sat. And Bonnie would never forget his expression.

And then something seared through Bonnie, bringing her to life, waking her to terror. She clutched at Meredith and stared around for the source. Something bad . . . something terrible was coming. Was almost here.

Stefan seemed to feel it, too. He was alert, stiff, like a wolf picking up a scent.

"What is it?" shouted Meredith. "What's wrong with you?"

"You've got to go!" Stefan rose, still holding the limp form in his arms. "Get out of here!"

"What do you mean? We can't leave you—"

"Yes, you can! Get out of here! Bonnie, get her out!"

No one had ever told Bonnie to take care of someone else before. People were always taking care of *her*. But now she seized Meredith's arm and began pulling. Stefan was right. There was nothing they could do for Elena, and if they stayed whatever had got her would get them.

"Stefan!" Meredith shouted as she was unaccountably dragged away.

"I'll put her under the trees. The willows, not the oaks," he called after them.

Why would he tell us that now? Bonnie wondered in some deep part of her mind that was not taken up with fear and the storm.

The answer was simple, and her mind promptly gave it back to her. Because he wasn't going to be around to tell them later.

CHAPTER

16

Long ago, in the dark side streets of Florence, starving, frightened, and exhausted, Stefan had made himself a vow. Several vows, in fact, about using the Powers he sensed within himself, and about how to treat the weak, blundering, but still-human creatures around him.

Now he was going to break them all.

He'd kissed Elena's cold forehead and laid her under a willow tree. He would come back here, if he could, to join her, after.

As he'd thought, the surge of Power had passed over Bonnie and Meredith and followed him, but it had receded again, and was now drawn back, waiting.

He wouldn't let it wait long.

Unencumbered by the burden of Elena's body, he broke into a predator's lope on the empty road. The freezing sleet and wind didn't bother him much. His hunter's senses pierced through them.

He turned them all to the task of locating the prey he wanted. No thinking of Elena now. Later, when this was over.

Tyler and his friends were still in the hut. Good. They never knew what was coming as the window burst into flying glass shards and the storm blew inside.

Stefan meant to kill when he seized Tyler by the neck and sank his fangs in. That had been one of his rules, not to kill, and he wanted to break it.

But another of the toughs came at him before he had quite drained Tyler of blood. The guy wasn't trying to protect his fallen leader, only to escape. It was his bad luck that his route took him across Stefan's path. Stefan flipped him to the ground and tapped the new vein eagerly.

The hot coppery taste revived him, warmed him, flowed through him like fire. It made him want more.

Power. Life. They had it; he needed it. With the glorious rush of strength that came with what he'd already drunk, he stunned them easily. Then he moved from one to another, drinking deep and throwing them away. It was like popping tops on a six-pack.

He was on the last when he saw Caroline huddling in the corner.

His mouth was dripping as he raised his head to look at her. Those green eyes, usually so narrow, showed white all around like those of a terrified horse.

Her lips were pale blurs as she gabbled soundless pleas.

He pulled her to her feet by the green sashes at her waist. She was moaning, her eyes rolling up in their sockets. He wound his hand in her auburn hair to position the exposed throat where he wanted it. His head reared back to strike – and Caroline screamed and went limp.

He dropped her. He'd had enough anyway. He was bursting with blood, like an overfed tick. He had never felt so strong, so charged with elemental power.

Now it was time for Damon.

He went out of the hut the same way he'd come in. But not in human form. A hunting falcon soared out the window and wheeled into the sky.

The new shape was wonderful. Strong . . . and cruel. And its eyes were sharp. It took him where he wanted, skimming over the oak trees of the woods. He was looking for a particular clearing.

He found it. Wind slashed at him but he spiralled downwards, with a keening scream of challenge. Damon, in human form below, threw up his hands to protect his face as the falcon dived at him.

Stefan ripped bloody strips out of his arms and heard Damon's answering scream of pain and anger.

I'm not your weak little brother any more. He sent the thought down to Damon on a stunning blast of Power. *And this time I've come for your blood.*

He felt the backwash of hatred from Damon, but the voice in his mind was mocking. *So this is the thanks I get for saving you and your betrothed?*

Stefan's wings folded and he dived again, his whole

world narrowed to one objective. Killing. He went for Damon's eyes, and the stick Damon had picked up whistled past his new body. His talons tore into Damon's cheek and Damon's blood ran. Good.

You shouldn't have left me alive, he told Damon. *You should have killed both of us at once.*

I'll be glad to correct the mistake! Damon had been unprepared before, but now Stefan could feel his drawing Power, arming himself, standing ready. *But first you might tell me whom I'm supposed to have killed this time.*

The falcon's brain could not deal with the riot of emotions the taunting question called up. Screaming wordlessly, it plummeted on Damon again, but this time the heavy stick struck home. Injured, one wing hanging, the falcon dropped behind Damon's back.

Stefan changed to his own form at once, scarcely feeling the pain of his broken arm. Before Damon could turn, he grabbed him, the fingers of his good hand digging into his brother's neck and spinning him around.

When he spoke, it was almost gently.

"Elena," he said, whispered, and went for Damon's throat.

It was dark, and very cold, and someone was hurt. Someone needed help.

But she was terribly tired.

Elena's eyelids fluttered and opened and that took care of the darkness. As for the cold . . . she was bone-cold, freezing, chilled to the marrow. And no wonder; there was ice all over her.

Somewhere, deep down, she knew it was more than that.

What had happened? She'd been at home, asleep – no, this was Founders' Day. She'd been in the cafeteria, on the stage.

Someone's face had looked funny.

It was too much to cope with; she couldn't think. Disembodied faces floated before her eyes, fragments of sentences sounded in her ears. She was very confused.

And so tired.

Better go back to sleep then. The ice wasn't really that bad. She started to lie down, and then the cries came to her again.

She heard them, not with her ears, but with her mind. Cries of anger and of pain. Someone was very unhappy.

She sat quite still, trying to sort it all out.

There was a quiver of movement at the edge of her vision. A squirrel. She could smell it, which was strange because she'd never smelled a squirrel before. It stared at her with one bright black eye and then it scampered up the willow tree. Elena realised she'd made a grab for it only when she came up empty with her fingernails digging into bark.

Now that was ridiculous. What on *earth* did she want a squirrel for? She puzzled over it for a minute, then lay back down, exhausted.

The cries were still going on.

She tried to cover her ears, but that did nothing to

block them out. Someone was hurt, and unhappy, and fighting. That was it. There was a fight going on.

All right. She'd figured it out. Now she could sleep.

She couldn't, though. The cries beckoned to her, drew her towards them. She felt an irresistible need to follow them to their source.

And *then* she could go to sleep. After she saw . . . him.

Oh, yes, it was coming back now. She remembered *him*. He was the one who understood her, who loved her. He was the one she wanted to be with for ever.

His face appeared out of the mists in her mind. She considered it lovingly. All right, then. For *him* she would get up and walk through this ridiculous sleet until she found the proper clearing. Until she could join him. Then they'd be together.

The very thought of him seemed to warm her. There was a fire inside him that few people could see. She saw it, though. It was like the fire inside her.

He seemed to be having some sort of trouble at the moment. At least, there was a lot of shouting. She was close enough to hear it with her ears as well as her mind now.

There, beyond that grandfather oak tree. That was where the noise was coming from. *He* was there, with his black, fathomless eyes, and his secret smile. And he needed her help. She would help him.

Shaking ice crystals out of her hair, Elena stepped into the clearing in the wood.

**Don't miss the exciting continuation of
The Vampire Diaries
Volume III: THE FURY**

CHAPTER

1

Elena stepped into the clearing.

Beneath her feet, tatters of autumn leaves were freezing into the slush. Dusk had fallen, and although the storm was dying away, the woods were getting colder. Elena didn't feel the cold.

Neither did she mind the dark. Her pupils opened wide, gathering up tiny particles of light that would have been invisible to a human. She could see the two figures struggling beneath the great oak tree quite clearly.

One had thick dark hair that the wind had churned into a tumbled sea of waves. He was slightly taller than the other, and although Elena couldn't see his face, she somehow knew his eyes were green.

The other had a shock of dark hair as well, but his was fine and straight, almost like the pelt of an animal.

His lips were drawn back from his teeth in fury, and the lounging grace of his body was gathered into a predator's crouch. His eyes were black.

Elena watched them for several minutes without moving. She'd forgotten why she had come here, why she'd been pulled here by the echoes of their battle in her mind. This close, the clamour of their anger and hatred and pain was almost deafening, like silent shouts coming from the fighters. They were locked in a death match.

I wonder which of them will win, she thought. They were both wounded and bleeding, and the taller one's left arm hung at an unnatural angle. Still, he had just slammed the other against the gnarled trunk of an oak tree. His fury was so strong that Elena could feel it and taste it as well as hear it, and she knew it was giving him impossible strength.

And then Elena remembered why she had come. How could she have forgotten? *He* was hurt. *His* mind had summoned her here, battering her with shockwaves of rage and pain. She had come to help him, because she belonged to him.

The two figures were down on the icy ground now, fighting like wolves, snarling. Swiftly and silently Elena went to them. The one with the wavy hair and green eyes – *Stefan*, a voice in her mind whispered – was on top, fingers scrabbling at the other's throat. Anger washed through Elena, anger and protectiveness. She reached between the two of them to grab that choking hand, to pry the fingers up.

It didn't occur to her that she shouldn't be strong

enough to do this. She *was* strong enough, that was all. She threw her weight to the side, wrenching her captive away from his opponent. For good measure she bore down hard on his wounded arm, knocking him flat on his face in the leaf-strewn slush. Then she began to choke him from behind.

Her attack had taken him by surprise, but he was far from beaten. He struck back at her, his good hand fumbling for her throat. His thumb dug into her windpipe.

Elena found herself lunging at the hand, going for it with her teeth. Her mind could not understand it, but her body knew what to do. Her teeth were a weapon, and they slashed into flesh, drawing blood.

But he was stronger than she was. With a jerk of his shoulders he broke her hold on him and twisted in her grasp, flinging her down. And then he was above her, his face contorted with animal fury. She hissed at him and went for his eyes with her nails, but he knocked her hand away.

He was going to kill her. Even wounded, he was by far the stronger. His lips had drawn back to show teeth already stained with scarlet. Like a cobra, he was ready to strike.

Then he stopped, hovering over her, his face changing.

Elena saw the green eyes widen. The pupils, which had been contracted to vicious dots, sprang open. He was staring down at her as if truly seeing her for the first time.

Why was he looking at her that way? Why didn't

he just get it over with? But now the iron hand on her shoulder was releasing her. The animal snarl had disappeared, replaced by a look of bewilderment and wonder. He sat back, helping her to sit up, all the while gazing into her face.

"Elena," he whispered, his voice cracking. "Elena, it's you."

Is that who I am? she thought. Elena?

It didn't really matter. She cast a glance towards the old oak tree. *He* was still there, standing between the upthrust roots, panting, supporting himself against it with one hand. *He* was looking at her with his endlessly black eyes, his brows drawn together in a frown.

Don't worry, she thought. I can take care of this one. He's stupid. Then she flung herself on the green-eyed one again.

"Elena!" he cried as she knocked him backwards. His good hand pushed at her shoulder, holding her up. "Elena, it's me, Stefan! Elena, look at me!"

She was looking. All she could see was the exposed patch of skin at his neck. She hissed again, upper lip drawing back, showing him her teeth.

He froze.

She felt the shock reverberate through his body, saw his gaze shatter. His face went as white as if someone had struck him a blow in the stomach. He shook his head slightly on the muddy ground.

"No," he whispered. "Oh, no . . ."

He seemed to be saying it to himself, as if he didn't expect her to hear him. He reached a hand towards her cheek and she snapped at it.

"Oh, Elena . . ." he whispered.

The last traces of fury, of animal bloodlust, had disappeared from his face. His eyes were dazed and stricken and grieving.

And vulnerable. Elena took advantage of the moment to dive for the bare skin at his neck. His arm came up to fend her off, to push her away, but then it dropped again.

He stared at her for a moment, the pain in his eyes reaching a peak, and then he simply gave up. He stopped fighting completely.

She could feel it happen, feel the resistance leave his body. He lay on the icy ground with scraps of oak leaves in his hair, staring up past her at the black and clouded sky.

Finish it, his weary voice said in her mind.

Elena hesitated for an instant. There was something about those eyes that called up memories inside her. Standing in the moonlight, sitting in an attic room . . . But the memories were too vague. She couldn't get a grasp on them, and the effort made her dizzy and sick.

And this one had to die, this green-eyed one called Stefan. Because he'd hurt *him*, the other one, the one Elena had been born to be with. No one could hurt *him* and live.

She clamped her teeth into his throat and bit deep.

She realised at once that she wasn't doing it quite right. She hadn't hit an artery or vein. She worried at the throat, angry at her own inexperience. It felt good to bite something but not much blood was coming. Frustrated, she lifted up and bit again, feeling his body jerk in pain.

Much better. She'd found a vein this time, but she hadn't torn it deeply enough. A little scratch like that wouldn't do. What she needed was to rip it right across, to let the rich hot blood stream out.

Her victim shuddered as she worked to do this, teeth raking and gnawing. She was just feeling the flesh give way when hands pulled at her, lifting her from behind.

Elena snarled without letting go of the throat. The hands were insistent, though. An arm looped about her waist, fingers twined in her hair. She fought, clinging on with teeth and nails to her prey.

Let go of him. Leave him!

The voice was sharp and commanding, like a blast from a cold wind. Elena recognised it and stopped struggling with the hands that pulled her away. As they deposited her on the ground and she looked up to see *him*, a name came into her mind. Damon. *His* name was Damon. She stared at him sulkily, resentful of being yanked away from her kill, but obedient.

Stefan was sitting up, his neck red with blood. It was running on to his shirt. Elena licked her lips, feeling a throb like a hunger pang, but which seemed to come from every fibre of her being. She was dizzy again.

"I thought," Damon said aloud, "that you said she was dead."

He was looking at Stefan, who was even paler than

before, if that were possible. That white face filled with infinite hopelessness.

"Look at her," was all he said.

A hand cupped Elena's chin, tilting her face up. She met Damon's narrowed dark eyes directly. Then long, slender fingers touched her lips, probing between them. Instinctively Elena tried to bite, but not very hard. Damon's finger found the sharp curve of a canine tooth and Elena did bite now, giving it a nip like a kitten's.

Damon's face was expressionless, his eyes hard.

"Do you know where you are?" he said.

Elena glanced around. Trees. "In the woods," she said craftily, looking back at him.

"And who is that?"

She followed his pointing finger. "Stefan," she said indifferently. "Your brother."

"And who am I? Do you know who I am?"

She smiled up at him, showing him her pointed teeth. "Of course I do. You're Damon, and I love you."

THE VAMPIRE DIARIES

L J Smith

0 340 84349 7	The Awakening	£4.99	❑
0 340 84350 0	The Struggle	£4.99	❑
0 340 84351 9	The Fury	£4.99	❑
0 340 84352 7	The Reunion	£4.99	❑

NIGHT WORLD

L J Smith

0 340 68751 7	Secret Vampire	£4.99	❑
0 340 68982 X	Daughters of Darkness	£4.99	❑
0 340 69001 1	Enchantress	£4.99	❑
0 340 69002 X	Dark Angel	£4.99	❑
0 340 69003 8	The Chosen	£4.99	❑
0 340 69004 6	Soulmate	£4.99	❑
0 340 70953 7	Huntress	£4.99	❑
0 340 70954 5	Black Dawn	£4.99	❑
0 340 70955 3	Witchlight	£4.99	❑

All Hodder Children's books are available at your local bookshop, or can be ordered direct from the publisher. Just tick the titles you would like and complete the details below. Prices and availability are subject to change without prior notice.

Please enclose a cheque or postal order made payable to *Bookpoint Ltd*, and send to: Hodder Children's Books, 39 Milton Park, Abingdon, OXON OX14 4TD, UK. Email Address: orders@bookpoint.co.uk

If you would prefer to pay by credit card, our call centre team would be delighted to take your order by telephone. Our direct line *01235 400414* (lines open 9.00 am–6.00 pm Monday to Saturday, 24 hour message answering service). Alternatively you can send a fax on *01235 400454*.

TITLE		FIRST NAME		SURNAME	

ADDRESS	

DAYTIME TEL:		POST CODE	

If you would prefer to pay by credit card, please complete:
Please debit my Visa/Access/Diner's Card/American Express (delete as applicable) card no:

Signature .... Expiry Date: ....

If you would NOT like to receive further information on our products please tick the box. ❑